THE SCARLET SLIPPER MYSTERY

Nancy meets Helene and Henri Fontaine, refugees from Centrovia who run a dancing school in River Heights. Strange circumstances have brought the brother and sister to the United States. When they receive an anonymous note threatening their lives, Nancy offers her help.

But she encounters nothing but puzzles. Are the Fontaines involved with the Centrovian underground? Have they been threatened by their own countrymen? Why? Is a series of paintings by Henri Fontaine being used for a sinister purpose?

Suddenly the Fontaines disappear. Have they been kidnapped? Nancy and her friends pursue the trail relentlessly, even though danger lurks around every corner. They are trapped by their enemies, and escape seems impossible. But Nancy's quick wit finally enables her to solve this intriguing and intricate mystery.

"Hannah!" Nancy cried. "Who did this to you?"

NANCY DREW MYSTERY STORIES

The Scarlet Slipper Mystery

BY CAROLYN KEENE

PUBLISHERS *Grosset & Dunlap* NEW YORK

Contents

The Scarlet Slipper Mystery

CHAPTER I

A Frightening Message

"WE will crash! Oh—oh!"

An ashen-faced, middle-aged man leaned across the aisle of the jet plane toward Nancy Drew.

The attractive reddish-blond girl smiled reassuringly. "Please don't worry," she said gently. "Only the engine has stopped. We'll be all right. And we'll soon reach River Heights."

"No! No!" the man moaned. "This is the end and all my work——!" He mumbled something to himself in a foreign tongue, then added, "My beloved Centrovia——" He shook a fist as if at the pilot, then buried his face in his hands.

When Nancy tried to comfort him further, a stewardess and a man and a woman passenger crowded alongside, blocking her view. The foreign gentleman quieted down, the two passengers returned to their seats, and Nancy became engrossed with the preparations for landing. Would it be as safe as she had predicted, she wondered?

The pilot maneuvered his ship expertly, bringing it down in a long glide and landing on the far end of the runway at the River Heights Airport.

When the plane rolled to a stop, Nancy smiled at the stranger across the aisle and said, "That wasn't bad, was it?"

"A miracle!" was the abrupt answer. The man stood up, grabbed a briefcase from under his seat, and quickly departed.

Nancy put on the jacket of her navy suit, picked up her purse, and walked slowly to the door. She paused to tell the stewardess how much she had enjoyed the flight, then hurried down the ramp. A short distance beyond stood her two closest friends, Bess Marvin and George Fayne, in gay cotton skirts and blouses.

George was an attractive girl with short dark hair and a slender figure, much like Nancy's. George's pretty cousin Bess, on the other hand, was slightly plump and worried continually about her figure.

"Hi, Nancy!" George exclaimed. "Have a good time at your Aunt Eloise's?"

"Perfect! I love New York."

"See any shows?" Bess asked.

Nancy nodded. "Three. One was a musical with wonderful dancing. You'd adore it, Bess."

As soon as Nancy had collected her baggage, the three girls walked to Nancy's convertible, which her friends had brought to the airport. Nancy took the wheel, and as they drove toward the residential section of town, she said, "Tell me everything that's happened while I was gone."

Bess giggled. "I've lost two pounds. There's a wonderful new dancing school in town, Nancy. All kinds of classes. I've joined one in reducing. Matter of fact, we just came from there."

George sniffed. "Yes, Bess takes it off dancing and puts it all back on by eating."

Nancy laughed and asked, "Who's running the new dancing school?"

Bess said that it was owned by a brother and sister named Henri and Helene Fontaine, who had recently come to River Heights from France, and that they were exceptionally fine dancers as well as excellent teachers.

"They have a simply delightful accent," Bess said. "Wait till you hear them talk."

George remarked that the classes had an interesting feature. Before each lesson, Helene and Henri gave a talk on the history of the dance.

"How fascinating!" said Nancy, her blue eyes sparkling. She was always intrigued by the background of any art form.

A few minutes later they reached the Fayne residence and George climbed out. She waved good-by, saying, "See you soon. I want to hear all about your trip, Nancy."

The car pulled away from the curb and Bess

suddenly cried out, "Oh, I've lost my purse. I must have left it at the dancing school in the excitement of going to meet you."

"We'll stop by and pick it up," Nancy offered.

The school occupied the second floor of an office building in the business section of River Heights. Nancy parked and waited while her friend hurried upstairs. Bess was back in a few seconds, however, without her purse.

"Oh, your pocketbook wasn't there after all?" Nancy asked.

"It's not that. I didn't even look for it. Nancy, something dreadful must have happened to Helene. She and Henri are there all alone, and Helene is crying as if her heart would break. Please come with me and see if we can help her."

Nancy hesitated a moment. She remarked that perhaps the matter was a family affair and they should not intrude. But Bess felt sure there was more to it than that.

"I heard Helene tell Henri she was so frightened!"

Nancy needed no further urging. She got out of the car instantly and hurried up the stairs with Bess. As the two girls entered the studio, Helene, a dainty, dark-haired girl, was saying to her brother in French, "No, we must flee again!"

Nancy and Bess stood still as the startled couple looked up. Henri was a tall, handsome young man with blond hair. He was leaning on an ivory-

and-gold French Provincial desk, behind which his sister was seated.

At a glance Nancy saw that the room was spacious and beautifully furnished with gold chairs and deep-blue drapes. On the wall above the desk hung a pair of scarlet ballet slippers.

"Oh, Bess, come in!" Helene urged, drying her eyes with a dainty handkerchief.

Bess moved forward slowly. She introduced Nancy, then added, "If you are in some kind of trouble, perhaps we can assist you. I couldn't help overhearing you when I came back for my handbag a few minutes ago."

The brother and sister exchanged quick glances. Then Henri slowly shook his head. "I'm afraid this is too serious a problem."

"Of course we don't mean to intrude," said Bess. "But you see, Nancy is a detective and has solved many difficult mysteries."

The Fontaines looked at Nancy in amazement. Then Henri said, "A girl detective? You are very pretty and—hardly look like a detective!"

Nancy laughed merrily. "I'm afraid Bess is giving me too much credit, but I'll be glad to do anything I can for you."

Again Henri and Helene exchanged glances. When the girl nodded to her brother, Henri said, "We do need a friend. Perhaps you girls are the ones to help us."

Henri took an unsigned note from his pocket

and showed it to Nancy. It was hand-printed in French and at the bottom, crudely drawn in red, was a pair of ballet slippers, similar to those hanging on the wall.

"The note was folded and left on the desk by some unknown person," he explained. "It was not addressed to Helene and me, but the scarlet-slippers insigne convinced us that the note was for us—no one else. Here, I will translate it for you."

Although Nancy could both read and speak French, she listened attentively as he began:

> You will lose your lives if you do not leave this area at once. Do not communicate with any friends you have made in the United States.

When Henri finished reading, Helene burst into tears. "I'm so afraid," she said. "This is the second note that we have received."

"Recently?" Nancy asked.

"No," Henri replied, and he went on to explain that the first note was sent to them in France about eighteen months before. That one had ordered the brother and sister to leave their country.

"Is that when you came here?" Nancy inquired.

"Yes, it was," Helene answered. Then, looking around furtively and lowering her voice, she added, "The other note also contained a threat. It said that the secret police from our native

"I'm so afraid," Helene said.

country were going to kidnap us and take us back there. I'm afraid that's what this one means."

"Isn't France your native country?" Bess broke in.

"No," Henri replied. "We are Centrovians."

"Centrovians!" Nancy exclaimed. "I wonder——"

As she stopped speaking, Helene asked if they had said anything to offend Nancy. The young detective said no. She was just startled because a short time before she had been talking with a man on a plane from New York who was a Centrovian.

"Oh!" the brother and sister cried out, and Henri added, "He was probably the one who left this note! What did he look like?"

Nancy described the man, adding that he was apparently a very nervous, excitable individual. The Fontaines failed to recognize him but were convinced that he was the guilty person.

"If this man is staying in River Heights, I ought to be able to find him," Nancy said.

The Fontaines begged her to do so. The girls rose to leave and Henri walked to the door with them.

"I have one very special request to make," he said. "We have never told anyone here that we came from Centrovia. France was our adopted country and we want it to be known that we came from there."

"I understand," said Nancy. "But perhaps you should tell me more about what happened and why you left Centrovia. I promise to keep everything confidential."

Henri related a terrifying tale of how Centrovia had been overrun by enemy forces. Due to the horrors of the occupation, many people had fled to other countries.

"This happened about eight years ago," the young man explained. "Our parents were among those who found refuge in France. Our name was Provak. When we reached Paris, we changed it to Fontaine."

Helene took up the story. "My parents—perhaps I should not tell you this—joined an organization that aimed to overthrow those new rulers in Centrovia. But both of them died before anything was accomplished." Helene pointed to the slippers on the wall. "Those belonged to my mother. She was a famous ballet dancer."

Henri put an arm about his sister's shoulders. "Our mother's death was caused by worry," he said. "When we fled from Centrovia, another family asked us to take a fortune in jewels with us to be used to help the underground movement. Unfortunately, the new rulers suspected this, and thus caused my parents a great deal of worry by accusing them of stealing the fortune and trying to make them reveal where it was."

"But they didn't steal it! They didn't!" Helene cried out. "The jewels were sold a few at a time to provide money for the work of freeing our people."

When the Fontaines stopped speaking, Nancy asked if there was any connection between the slippers on the note and those on the wall.

"I don't know," Helene answered. "Oh, what do you think we should do? Obey the warning and give up our work here?"

It was several seconds before Nancy replied. Then she said, "Please don't make any hasty decisions. I'm sure I can help you. Furthermore, my father is a lawyer and I'll talk to him."

The Fontaines agreed to delay leaving.

"Surely whoever sent the warning note would not expect you to wind up your business affairs on a moment's notice," Nancy added. "In the meantime, I may find a way out for you."

"Oh, thank you," said Helene. "You are a true friend and, just think, we have known you only a few minutes. May I call you Nancy?"

The young detective smiled at Helene's charming old-world manners and said that from now on they would be Helene and Nancy to each other.

"And will you please call me Henri?" Helene's brother asked, a twinkle in his eyes.

Nancy eagerly agreed.

Bess retrieved her purse and a short time later the girls said good-by to the Fontaines. Nancy promised to get in touch with them the next day.

As they drove along the main street, Bess asked about the stranger in the plane who was from Centrovia. The words were hardly out of her mouth when, at an intersection, a man suddenly stepped from the curb, directly into the path of the car.

Nancy slammed on her brakes so fast that the tires screeched. Instantly the man leaped back to the sidewalk and she cried, "Bess, take the wheel! That's the Centrovian I met on the plane. I must talk to him!"

Before Bess could object, Nancy was out of the car and hurrying toward the stranger.

CHAPTER II

Mysteries Multiply

As Nancy bounded around the front of her car, the traffic light changed. The automobile in the right lane rounded the corner, cutting off her dash to the curb. By the time she reached the sidewalk, the man she was chasing had disappeared.

Bess parked the convertible and watched as Nancy dodged in and out of nearby stores, looking for the stranger. Finally the young sleuth returned and climbed into her car.

"That man certainly vanished suddenly," she said. "But I intend to find him."

Nancy was greatly admired in River Heights because of her unusual ability to track down elusive clues, as well as her courage and quick-wittedness.

The girl's reputation as a detective went back to the time when her father, a prominent lawyer, had turned over to her the case known as *The Secret of the Old Clock*. Since then, Nancy had been engaged in countless adventures. Recently she had finished working on a strange circus intrigue—*The Ringmaster's Secret*.

Now she was eager to solve the Fontaines' mystery and was annoyed that the first good lead in the case had slipped through her fingers.

Bess, still at the wheel, drove to her house. She alighted and said she would see Nancy the next day. "Please be careful," she added as the young detective drove away.

Nancy headed home, a spacious dwelling on a street lined with old sycamores. She parked in the winding, flower-bordered driveway.

As she hurried up the walk to the kitchen door, Hannah Gruen, the Drews' housekeeper, came out to meet her. Nancy embraced the pleasant-faced woman who had lived with the family since Mrs. Drew's death many years before.

Nancy's little terrier, Togo, barked sharply and bounded to greet her. She caught him up in her arms, then turned to the housekeeper. "How is everything? Is Dad home?"

"Things are fine," Hannah replied. "Here comes your father now."

At that moment Carson Drew pulled into the driveway. Nancy ran to greet him. He was a tall, handsome man. Nancy loved his pleasant disposition, the twinkle in his eyes, and his keen mind.

During dinner, Nancy told Hannah and her father about her trip. Then she mentioned the Fontaines and their problem.

"It sounds very serious," Mr. Drew said. "I'd rather you did nothing about this until I consult government authorities on the subject. I'm flying down to Washington this evening."

Nancy nodded. "But may I search for that mysterious man who was on the plane?"

"All right," the lawyer conceded, "but be careful. If necessary, get the police."

After dinner Nancy began telephoning local hotels. But no one known to be from Centrovia was registered at any of them.

At nine o'clock a taxi came to take Mr. Drew to the airport. He had been gone only a few minutes when the doorbell rang.

"Oh, how do you do, Mrs. Boyd," Nancy said, greeting a slender, gray-haired woman, who was red-faced and seemed upset.

"I want to see your father right away, Nancy."

"I'm sorry, but he's not at home. Can I do anything for you?"

"Well, I don't know," Mrs. Boyd answered as Nancy led her into the living room. "It's about Mr. Howard, down at the jewelry store. I think I ought to sue him!"

The distraught woman settled down in a comfortable chair. "This morning when I was in the store," she went on, "I saw a bisque figurine that appealed to me. It was expensive, but I bought it. After I got home, what do you think? There was a long crack in the little statue."

From her handbag Mrs. Boyd lifted a dancing-girl figurine. Inspecting it closely, Nancy could see a flaw that ran along a fold in the skirt.

"When I saw it," said Mrs. Boyd, "I took the piece right back to Mr. Howard. And he refused to return my money! He implied that I had damaged the statue after I left the store. Now, what do you think, Nancy? Shouldn't I sue him?"

The young detective wanted to hear Mr. Howard's side of the story before answering the question.

"Mrs. Boyd, I think my father will have to decide that," she replied hesitantly. "But, in the meantime, suppose I take the statue down to the store and talk to Mr. Howard? Perhaps we can straighten this out."

"Oh, thank you, my dear," said Mrs. Boyd gratefully as she rose to leave. "Maybe you can talk some sense into Mr. Howard."

The next morning Nancy arrived at the jewelry store soon after it opened. Mr. Howard was standing behind a counter near the door.

Nancy showed him the figurine and told him about Mrs. Boyd's complaint. Mr. Howard looked annoyed. "I didn't think that crack was bad enough for me to have to take the figurine back," he said.

"Perhaps not," Nancy said. "But it does look as if the figurine had been tampered with, and I'm sure Mrs. Boyd didn't do it."

Mr. Howard got a magnifying glass and studied the statue. He admitted that Nancy's suspicion might be right. With a thin knifelike instrument, he deepened the crack a tiny bit. The figurine fell apart in his hands!

"Well, for Pete's sake!" Mr. Howard cried. "I wonder if the rest are this way!"

The jeweler went to the rear of his shop, where five other statuettes were standing on a shelf. "Every figurine has the same flaw," he announced after examining them. "I'll call the company that sold me these."

Nancy watched as the jeweler telephoned the New York firm. Finally, he grew pale and said, "You mean you have no salesman named Warte? But he showed me his business card!"

Nancy guessed that Mr. Howard had been cheated by an impostor.

"What am I going to do?" the jeweler cried despairingly, as he hung up.

The young sleuth expressed her sympathy and said she was afraid there was nothing he could do. "What did the man look like?" she asked.

Mr. Howard said the salesman was about five foot eight and pale, with graying hair and deep-set eyes.

"He was some salesman," the jeweler went on. "He had an accent. He dropped French and German phrases into his conversation. Talked about the figurines as a foreign art dealer might."

Nancy advised Mr. Howard to notify the police. "I suspect the flaws are not just evidence of poor workmanship," she said. On a sudden hunch, she added, "Would you sell these figurines to me at a reasonable price?"

Mr. Howard shrugged. "The lot for five dollars."

"Fine," Nancy said. "And now, Mr. Howard, will you please take them apart for me?"

"Of course," he said. "Why?"

"I think we may find something inside one of them," said Nancy. "Mr. Warte probably wanted to get rid of these figurines in a hurry. The reason may be hidden inside them."

Mr. Howard halved the first figurine. "Nothing in here."

The next three bisque dancing girls contained no clue. But as the last came apart, Nancy and Mr. Howard gasped in amazement.

Inside lay a small piece of paper with a number on it. 10561-B-24!

"That can't be a manufacturer's number," Nancy declared. "If it were, it wouldn't have been sealed inside the statuette."

Tucking the paper into her handbag, the young

detective asked Mr. Howard if he would glue the figurines back together. She would return for them later.

"And don't you think," she said, smiling, "that you ought to refund Mrs. Boyd's money now?"

"By all means," the jeweler conceded.

Later that day, when Mr. Drew returned from the capital, his daughter told him about the figurines, the impostor, and the strange number. The lawyer complimented her for having settled the matter so quickly and satisfactorily.

Nancy asked her father what he had learned about the Fontaine case in Washington.

"No adverse reports have ever come in on the couple," he answered. "The authorities will look into the matter from the foreign angle. We have permission to take care of the situation here."

"Good!" Nancy said. "Let's begin at once."

Mr. Drew smiled. "What do you suggest?"

"Dad, I'd like to bring the Fontaines here until the mystery is solved. Then I'd know they were safe."

Hannah Gruen, overhearing, threw up her hands. "Nancy Drew, that's asking for trouble!"

The lawyer agreed, but after some coaxing, Nancy won them both over by promising to keep the secret from all but their closest friends.

She telephoned the Fontaines at once. The brother and sister discussed Nancy's offer. Henri

told her they would like to accept but were re-
luctant to close the dancing school.

"I don't think that will be necessary," said
Nancy. "We'll think of a solution to that problem this evening. I'll pick you up in front of the
school at ten o'clock."

When Nancy returned to the living room, she
found that Bess and George had dropped in. Mr.
Drew was telling them of the new plan.

Nancy related her conversation with the Fontaines, and the girls discussed how the dancing
school might be kept in operation. Suddenly Bess
beamed. "I know a number of dancing teachers
in town! I'm sure I could get them to conduct
some of the classes."

Bess made several quick telephone calls and
soon announced, "All the older classes are taken
care of. But I couldn't find anyone for the small
children."

Nancy's face lighted up. "Why don't you and
I teach them?" she suggested.

Bess was thrilled. She had taken lessons since
she was a tiny tot and knew all the steps that were
taught to small children. Nancy, too, had studied
dancing and was quite accomplished.

"Hypers!" said sports-loving George. "I'm glad
you didn't ask me to do any teaching!"

"Now we ought to have a manager," said Bess.

"Maybe Ned will have a suggestion," Nancy

said. "He thought he might stop by this evening on his way back to the summer camp where he's a counselor."

A few minutes later tall, dark-haired Ned Nickerson arrived. "Hello, everybody! Any new mysteries?"

"A couple," Nancy admitted.

George looked mischievous. "In connection with one of them," she said, "we need a manager for a dancing school. Are you qualified?"

The athletic youth grinned. "Why, of course!" he declared, striking a ballet pose.

Bess giggled. "We're serious, Ned. We have to find a manager." She explained the situation.

Ned looked thoughtful. Then he said, "I think perhaps my mother could help out."

"Wonderful!" Nancy cried. She telephoned Mrs. Nickerson and was delighted when the kind woman accepted, promising to be at the dancing school early the next morning.

After Nancy had told Ned about the case in detail, the tall youth glanced at his wristwatch and declared it was time to leave. "I'm due at a counselors' meeting late this evening," he said. "I'll be seeing you soon. Please be careful, Nancy," he added, squeezing her hand.

Bess and George said they would be back after dinner to help Nancy plan the best way to move the Fontaines into the Drew home.

When the cousins returned two hours later, George announced that they had an idea. "We'll patrol the street," she explained.

"We'll steer any suspicious persons away from the house," Bess went on. "And if a troublemaker should appear as you approach, we'll wave a white handkerchief to warn you."

"A good idea," Nancy agreed.

George asked Nancy for a full description of the mysterious stranger she suspected of sending the threatening note to the Fontaines.

"Suppose we see him. Shall we call a policeman?" the adventurous girl asked, relishing the excitement.

"If there's one around," replied Nancy. "Of course, we don't know that this man is guilty. If you see him, it would be best simply to use some ruse to get him out of the way until after the Fontaines are safely in the house."

Nancy said that she had arranged with the pilot of a private plane to fly the couple from River Heights to another airport. They would return by train, and she would pick them up at the River Heights station.

"In the meantime, I'll come back here," she said. "If I'm delayed, I'll phone."

Shortly before ten o'clock, Nancy drove off. Bess and George stationed themselves on each side of the street.

After some time had elapsed, Bess saw a vaguely familiar figure coming up the sidewalk. He looked like the suspected stranger!

Bess crossed the street and summoned her cousin. It was almost time for Nancy to return, and the fellow was too close to the Drew home for safety!

George had a sudden inspiration. She calculated the distance so that she and Bess would pass the man under a street light, where they could pretend to recognize him.

When they walked by him, George turned back and said, "Why, aren't you from Centrovia?"

The man looked at her in amazement. "Yes, I am. Why do you ask?"

"I've been searching everywhere for you," George answered glibly. "I'm a reporter for the local paper, and I'd like to interview you for a feature story. Won't you come with me to the hotel coffee shop and tell me about the fabulous life you've led?"

"But I don't want a story about me in the newspaper," the man protested.

"It will be a marvelous human interest item," George persisted.

Suddenly the man scowled. "Say, what's going on here?" he asked harshly. "If you don't mind your own business, I'll call the police."

He strode off in the opposite direction and was lost to view.

Suddenly the cousins realized that it was after eleven o'clock and Nancy had not yet arrived. They waited another twenty minutes. Still no sign of Nancy.

Finally Bess decided to go into the house to find out if Nancy had telephoned.

Hannah Gruen answered her knock. The housekeeper was wringing her hands in dismay. "Oh, Bess," the woman wailed. "I haven't heard from Nancy! I just know something has happened to her!"

CHAPTER III

A Worrisome Ride

WHEN Nancy parked in front of the Fontaines' dancing school, Henri and his sister were waiting for her. They had several suitcases with them. Anyone spying on the dancers would think they were going on a long trip.

Nancy whispered her new plan to the couple and they nodded assent. "None of your enemies will be able to learn your destination in a private plane," she said.

"That's splendid." Henri smiled.

There was little traffic and they soon reached the River Heights Airport. Nancy parked, then pointed to the waiting plane, which belonged to a friend of Ned Nickerson's. The Fontaines thanked Nancy profusely and hurried off, whispering that they would see her soon.

As Nancy waited to wave good-by to her new friends, she became aware of a man not far away who stared alternately at her and then at the waiting plane. She wondered whether he was merely an idle bystander or a spy connected with the Fontaine mystery.

The man, who was slender and of medium height, had black hair and flushed cheeks. His eyes were penetrating, and Nancy found herself turning from his insolent stare.

After she had waved good-by and the plane was airborne, Nancy turned to look at the man again. He was gone! At first she felt relieved; then her mind began to race. He might be making inquiries about the plane's destination from some mechanic who had not been warned against giving out the information! The spy could telephone some member of the group and arrange to have him meet the Fontaines with a phony message, getting them into real trouble.

Nancy tried to shake off the mood. "I'm making a mountain out of a molehill," she said to herself. "Just the same, I'll look around."

She did not find the man and finally concluded he had left the airport. Her search had taken half an hour and by that time the Fontaines had completed their plane trip and would soon board a train for the return journey.

"I won't have time to go home," Nancy decided. "I'll take a circuitous route to the River Heights station to throw anyone off my trail."

Nancy had gone only a mile when she noticed

a car following her. She increased her speed, and the driver behind her did the same.

"Oh, dear," Nancy thought, "this may mean trouble!"

On the spur of the moment she decided to switch to a side road with many curves. It was just around the next bend, and by hurrying Nancy knew she could turn into it before the other car reached the curve. Turning off the convertible's headlights, Nancy hoped that the driver trailing her would not suspect her ruse.

Unfortunately the side road was rutted and bumpy, and she was forced to slow down, with the result that the pursuing driver spotted the convertible's brake lights and came after her. Nancy rolled up the windows and locked the doors. She drove as fast as she dared, but the other car finally overtook the convertible and forced it so close to a ditch that she was compelled to stop.

From behind the wheel climbed the sinister-looking man she had suspected of being a spy at the airport! He came to stand beside her window.

"You're Miss Drew?" he asked with a decided French accent.

Nancy did not reply.

"I am a friend of the Fontaines," the man said brusquely. "Where are they going?"

Still, Nancy did not answer. The man shook his fist at her. "If you do not tell me, it will go badly with you. You are playing a dangerous game, mademoiselle."

Nancy's heart was pounding, but her voice was calm as she said, "I have nothing to say. Please move your car out of the way!"

"I will not!" the man cried. "You're going to answer my question or——"

He stopped speaking because suddenly he was outlined in the headlights of a car coming up behind them. Apparently fearful of being caught, the man hurried back to his car and got in. But he called back, "You haven't heard the last of this!"

He geared his car and roared away. The approaching automobile slowed down. A young couple was in it, and the girl called anxiously to Nancy, "Are you all right?"

"Yes," Nancy assured her. "But I'd like to follow you into River Heights, if you don't mind."

"Okay."

On the way Nancy wondered if her well-laid plan might be falling through and the stranger would pick up her trail again. But no car followed. Finally she reached the railroad station and parked in the shadows across the street as prearranged with the Fontaines.

"Hannah and the girls must be wondering where I am," Nancy thought. "I wish I dared leave the car and phone them. Here's hoping the train won't be late and delay me any longer."

Presently it loomed down the tracks. Nancy looked around for suspicious persons who might be watching, but the station area seemed to be deserted. The engine ground to a halt and a few passengers alighted. The Fontaines climbed down from the last coach. Henri's hat was pulled low and the scarf on Helene's head obscured her face.

They found the car quickly, got into the front seat without saying a word, as formerly agreed upon, and Nancy drove off. After they had gone two blocks, Henri said, "Did everything go all right with you?"

Nancy did not want to frighten the couple, but she felt that they should know every detail of the case, and so she told them what had happened.

Helene gasped. "Oh, Nancy, our enemies mean to harm us, even though we tried to make them think we obeyed their command!"

"Perhaps not. They may want to know where you are only to be sure you're not planning to return to River Heights," Nancy said reassuringly.

She described the man, but neither Henri nor Helene could identify him as anyone they had known in France or had met in the United States.

As Nancy turned into her own street, she noticed a man just barely visible in the shadows.

He was strolling on the sidewalk opposite the Drew home and looked suspicious. There was no sign of Bess or George. Fearful that the man might be a spy, Nancy drove around the block.

When she returned, the man was not in sight. Nancy sighed with relief when she spotted Bess and George standing in the driveway, motioning for her to enter. Mr. Drew met the group at the garage. When Nancy mentioned her suspicion about the spy, her father said that he had been the man strolling opposite their house. He was relieving her friends for a few minutes. Along with Hannah and the girls, he had been fearful for Nancy's safety.

The Fontaines were introduced and escorted into the house. There they met Hannah Gruen, who threw her arms around Nancy. When Nancy explained the reason for her long absence, the housekeeper visibly shuddered and Bess cried, "Oh, Nancy, I knew this would be a dangerous case!"

The Fontaines looked very uncomfortable and Bess regretted her remark. She apologized, explaining she had not meant it the way it sounded. There was danger for all concerned and she hoped the mystery would be solved soon.

To cover the embarrassment, Hannah, who had drawn all the drapes, invited everyone to share a midnight snack of sandwiches and milk she had prepared. As they ate, the young people relaxed. Half an hour later Mr. Drew drove Bess and George home.

Helene was shown to a guest room on the second floor by Nancy, and Henri was taken to one on the third by Hannah. Over and over the Fontaines expressed their great gratitude. Nancy and Hannah, in turn, said they hoped that the brother and sister would be comfortable and happy during their stay.

"And don't be bashful about asking for anything you want," the kindly housekeeper added.

At breakfast the following day Helene said she had her first request. In the excitement of the sudden move she had forgotten about a coaching job she had undertaken.

"It's the big charity show to be given in the Civic Center," Helene explained. "Nancy, would you mind getting in touch with Mrs. Parsons, the chairwoman, and telling her I will have to give up the coaching? I suggest that she get one of the other teachers in town to replace me."

Nancy knew Mrs. Parsons and said she would stop at her home on the way to the dancing school. At nine-thirty she rang the bell at the Parsons' home.

"Good morning, Nancy," the woman said, and invited her caller in. After Nancy had relayed Helene's message, Mrs. Parsons exclaimed, "Oh, dear, the whole show is falling apart! First I lose my solo dancer; now my coach is resigning!"

"I'm sorry," said Nancy sympathetically. "But surely one of the other teachers in town can help you out."

"Maybe. But you know how it is. Nobody wants to be second fiddle," Mrs. Parsons said. "But that doesn't bother me as much as losing my prize dancer. Nancy, she's marvelous!"

"Who is she?" Nancy asked.

"Millie Koff. She and her father were staying at the Claymore Hotel. They didn't expect to leave for some time. Then late last night they checked out with no explanation."

Mrs. Parsons paused a moment, then said, "Nancy, I'm going to tell you a little secret. I have an idea the Koffs may be in some kind of trouble. Millie once confided in me that she had come to this country from Centrovia and ——"

"Centrovia!" Nancy echoed, startled.

CHAPTER IV

A Vicious Caller

"Oh, please tell me more about the Koffs!" Nancy begged Mrs. Parsons.

"Well, I don't know much, my dear," she replied. "Mr. Koff is a writer—he's a very eccentric, excitable person. He and his daughter Millie have been staying at the Claymore Hotel. She is a talented dancer, so we asked her to perform in the charity show. I believe she studied abroad."

A physical description of Mr. Koff fitted the man who had sat across the aisle from Nancy during the plane trip. She asked Mrs. Parsons if she might use her telephone, and when the woman nodded, Nancy called the Claymore Hotel.

During other cases on which she had worked, Nancy had become acquainted with the manager. After identifying herself, she asked for the forwarding address of the Koffs.

"I'm sorry, Nancy," the manager replied, "but they did not leave one. Are they involved in some mystery?"

"Possibly," Nancy said. "If any word comes from them, will you please notify me?"

The manager assured her that he would. When Nancy told Mrs. Parsons about the conversation, the woman shook her head in disappointment and said she would have to find a substitute for Millie.

"How about your taking the part?" she asked.

Nancy laughed. "You flatter me, Mrs. Parsons. I'd be glad to help you out with some of the dancing, but please don't put me in as a soloist. I haven't had much time for any ballet dancing in recent years."

"But you still dance exceedingly well," said the chairwoman of the charity show. "And I'm sure you could learn the speaking part easily."

There was no talking Mrs. Parsons out of her idea. She was flustered and concerned. Not only had she lost Millie Koff as soloist but also Helene Fontaine as coach. The woman began pacing the floor.

"All right, Mrs. Parsons," Nancy said. "I'll do the best I can for you. But if Millie Koff comes back, I'll bow out."

From a desk Mrs. Parsons produced a script for the performance. Flipping over several pages, she came to the scene in which Millie Koff was to have appeared. She and Nancy sat down and went over the part together. When they had finished, Nancy admitted that there was not much to the role, and she could quickly learn the speaking part. She, herself, would have to develop the dance act.

With a copy of the script and a record under her arm, Nancy hurried off, promising to report for rehearsal that afternoon. Already behind schedule, she found Ned Nickerson's mother waiting for her outside the door of the Fontaines' dancing school.

Nancy walked up to her, smiling, and said, "Good morning, Mrs. Nickerson. I'm sorry I'm late."

Mrs. Nickerson looked very pretty, she thought, with her prematurely white wavy hair, her petite figure, and her stylishly tailored cotton dress.

As Nancy unlocked the door, she said, "Mrs. Nickerson, the Fontaines want me to tell you how much they appreciate what you're doing."

Mrs. Nickerson said she was glad to be included and hoped that something exciting would happen. She and Nancy spent an hour together, checking the schedule of classes and going through the registration cards to become acquainted with the pupils.

When everything was ready, Nancy found that

she would be free for half an hour before her first class. She decided to start work on the dance she would perform in the benefit show.

Nancy found a leotard in her size and put it on in the dressing room. Then she walked into the large practice room, which had mirrors on three walls.

"First I'll listen to the record that Millie Koff was going to use," Nancy decided. She placed the "Satiric Polka," by Shostakovich, on the turntable and flicked on the switch.

As the music filled the room, Nancy shut her eyes and let her feet and body move naturally to the distinctive rhythm.

"Of course I haven't the same ballet technique as Millie," she thought, "but I'll improvise to the music, combining ballet and rhythmic modern dancing. That should do the trick."

She played the record over several times until her choreography had formed a regular pattern. Realizing that her movements betrayed her love for mystery, Nancy suddenly found herself giggling. Her dance had become a graceful chase portraying the conflict between someone being pursued and the pursuer!

"I'll need a lot of practice," Nancy said to herself, as she performed the final leap with an intricate turn.

Nancy heard several pupils arriving for their

class and hurried into the dressing room to change to street clothes. The substitute teacher arrived and everything went well.

Nancy and Mrs. Nickerson had luncheon together; then Nancy borrowed the leotard again and left for the charity-show rehearsal at the Civic Center. She went at once to the auditorium, where several of the performers were on stage, talking to Mrs. Parsons.

Among them was a man who now turned and came down the steps. As he hurried toward a side door, Nancy looked at him in amazement.

He was the man who had stopped her on the country road!

As quickly as she could, Nancy ran across the back of the auditorium and down the last aisle toward the exit he had taken. When she reached the corridor, he was not in sight.

A porter mopping the floor told her that a man had left through a nearby door. She dashed outside and up an alley to the street. But by the time Nancy reached it, the man had disappeared.

For several minutes she watched the passing cars, hoping that the man might have parked and would drive by. But her hopes were in vain and in disappointment she returned to the auditorium and donned the leotard.

Mrs. Parsons introduced her to the other players and told them that Nancy would take the part Millie Koff had planned to play.

"I think we'll go over that first," Mrs. Parsons said.

She explained that Nancy had been given the part only that morning, but she was sure she would do well. Nancy hoped so, and was not displeased with her performance, although she realized it could be improved.

When her part in the rehearsal was over, she walked up to Mrs. Parsons and asked about the man who had been in the auditorium a short time before.

"I don't know his name," Mrs. Parsons replied. "He came in here to ask about Helene Fontaine."

Mrs. Parsons explained that he was very eager to find the young dancing-school teacher and wanted her address.

"Of course I couldn't give it to him," said Mrs. Parsons. "He acted as if he did not believe me and went off in a huff."

Nancy asked some of the performers who were standing around if they knew who he was, but no one did.

"He must be a stranger in town," Nancy decided, as she put her street clothes over her leotard and left the auditorium. "I wonder if he is really a friend of the Fontaines."

Nancy returned to the dancing school and learned from Mrs. Nickerson that everything had been going smoothly.

"Nothing has happened in connection with the

mystery," she reported. "Nancy, I'm dreadfully sorry, but I'll have to leave right away. I almost forgot an engagement I had made previously. It's too late now to break it. Would you be able to take over for the rest of the afternoon?"

"Oh, certainly," said Nancy.

"I'll be in first thing tomorrow morning," Mrs. Nickerson promised.

Nancy thanked her and sat down at the receptionist's desk. A few minutes after Mrs. Nickerson had gone, Bess arrived to teach a class of little girls.

"Hello, Nancy," she said. "Any news?"

Nancy told her about the man at the auditorium. Bess shivered, and again warned Nancy to be careful.

"Well, there's one place I'm sure I'll be safe," said Nancy with a chuckle. "That's right here in the dancing school. I'm going to stay the rest of the afternoon and evening."

Bess heaved a sigh. "You know, I'm scared silly to take this class. I've never taught dancing in my life."

Nancy tried to reassure her friend as Bess went into the dressing room. About twenty minutes later she peeked into the big room. The little ballerinas were paying strict attention. It was amusing to watch them try to imitate Bess.

As Nancy returned to the desk, a woman hurried into the reception room. She was a coarse-looking person, wearing too much makeup and a strong, pungent perfume. She was dressed in a flowered red-and-green dress, and a red hat was perched on her disheveled reddish curls.

"Where is Helene Fontaine?" the woman asked abruptly.

"Miss Fontaine is not here right now," Nancy replied.

"I'm Mrs. Judson," the woman said tartly. "Helene is a good friend of mine. I've heard she left town. The idea of her going without telling me! What's her address?"

"I'm afraid I can't give it to you," said Nancy.

Mrs. Judson cried in a loud voice, "That's ridiculous! Helene wouldn't run off without telling somebody here at the school where she was going." She stamped her foot angrily. "I demand to know where Helene and Henri Fontaine are!"

"I cannot tell you, Mrs. Judson!" Nancy said firmly, her eyes flashing.

The woman began a tirade, shouting that Nancy had no right to keep the information from her. Finally Nancy could take the abuse no longer. She rose from the desk and went around to escort Mrs. Judson outside.

"There are children here," she said, "and we can't have a disturbance."

Mrs. Judson glowered as Nancy took her arm

and led her out to the stairway. Suddenly Mrs. Judson shook herself free of Nancy's grasp, turned halfway around, and jammed her elbow hard into the girl's hip.

Nancy lost her balance. She reached frantically for the banister, missed, and pitched headlong down the steps!

CHAPTER V

Clue of the Stamp

THE stairway was steep. Waving her arms wildly in an attempt to save herself, Nancy fell all the way to the bottom. She lay there, stunned.

Mrs. Judson rushed down the steps, stepped over Nancy, and hurried out the doorway!

Shocked and angry, Nancy was sure that Mrs. Judson was no friend of the Fontaines. The girl stood up, but when she put her weight on her right ankle, she winced with pain and fell back on the step, her face pale.

At this moment George Fayne burst through the door. Seeing Nancy, she cried anxiously, "Hypers! What happened to you?"

"I'll be all right," Nancy said, "but follow the woman who just went out the door. I must know who she is and where she lives!"

George waited for no further explanation.

Hurrying to the sidewalk, she spotted the suspect running up the block.

Meanwhile, Nancy hopped up the stairway on her left foot, clutching the banister rail with both hands. As she reached the reception room, Bess, just dismissing a class, saw her.

"Nancy, you're hurt!" she cried.

After the children had left, Nancy told her what had happened. Bess was furious.

"That awful person!" she exclaimed. "Nancy, you're hurt more than you admit. Come into the dressing room and let me look at your ankle."

She took off Nancy's shoe, put cold compresses on the swollen ankle, then bound it. By the time George returned, the pain had eased.

Nancy turned and asked, "Any luck?"

"Yes and no," George replied. "I followed the woman to the post office. She went to the General Delivery window and asked for mail for Judson."

George said that the clerk had handed Mrs. Judson a letter that had seemed to disturb her greatly.

"She got red in the face and I thought she was going to cry. She stuffed the letter and part of the envelope into her handbag," the girl went on. "But the other piece of the envelope with the stamp on it fell to the floor and I picked it up as she left."

"Good!" said Nancy.

"But my luck ended there." George sighed.

"Nancy, you're hurt!" Bess exclaimed.

"Mrs. Judson rushed outside and got into a taxi. I couldn't find another one, so I had no way of following her. And I didn't even get the license number of the cab."

Nancy examined the thin piece of envelope George had saved. The letter had been post-marked in Paris, France, and sent by airmail. The notation *Par Avion* had been written by hand.

George suggested that she drive Nancy home and then return to help Bess. "I'll take over the reception desk," she promised her friend. "You don't need a ballet dancer there!"

On the way home, the girls stopped at Dr. Milton's office. He said that Nancy had suffered only a mild strain. He strapped the ankle and assured her that if she stayed off it as much as possible, it should be good as new in a day or two.

When Nancy reached home, Hannah Gruen was distraught. "That dancing school isn't worth it!" she declared loudly.

At that, Henri and Helene rushed down the stairs. When they heard what had happened, Helene said, "Nancy, I had no idea that you would get into trouble. We cannot permit it to continue. Our enemies are more dangerous than I thought."

Nancy had grown very fond of the dancing couple. Besides, she was determined not to give up so easily. Smiling, she insisted that her accident was of little consequence.

Before the Fontaines had a chance to comment further, Nancy asked them if they knew Mrs. Judson or had ever heard of her. They said no. Thinking the woman might be using an assumed name, Nancy described her carefully. The dancers said they knew no such person.

Nancy showed the couple the piece of envelope with the French stamp and asked if the Fontaines recognized the handwriting. They did not.

As Nancy ran her fingernail over the strange stamp, something on the envelope caught her eye. "Hannah," she said to the housekeeper, "will you please steam the stamp off this envelope for me?"

The housekeeper went to the kitchen and returned quickly. Wide-eyed she exclaimed, "It beats me how Nancy figures things out!"

"I had a clue," Nancy admitted. "I noticed a dot of ink extending beyond the edge of the stamp."

"Well, it was a good idea," said Hannah. "There was a number under the stamp."

"What is it?" the three asked eagerly.

Dramatically, Hannah read, "10561-B-24!"

It was the same number that Nancy had found inside the bisque figurine!

Astonished, Nancy told them about the statuette and the impostor who had sold it to the local jeweler. "Does the number mean anything to either of you?" she asked Henri and Helene.

They shook their heads. "Could it be some sort of a code?" Henri asked.

"Perhaps," Nancy admitted. "And it may be in French. Let's see if we can figure it out. Have you ever tried solving a cryptogram?"

"A few times," Helene answered.

"Good. Now, if Hannah will bring us a pad of paper and some pencils, we'll all work on it. I'll work in English and you two can experiment in French."

They tried simple substitutions, using the series of numbers for letters of the alphabet, but nothing came of this. Next they tried transposition, numbering the alphabet with *z* for *1* and *a* for *26*.

"I believe we've been following the wrong trail," Nancy said finally, after several leads had failed to produce a message. "This may even be a serial number of some sort."

Hannah Gruen, who had been listening, declared she thought enough decoding had been done that day. "Nancy, I suggest that you go to bed and let me serve supper to you in your room."

Helene and Henri backed Hannah up, urging Nancy to rest her ankle. She finally consented.

The young detective went to sleep early that night. She woke the next morning eager to continue work.

When she hopped down to breakfast, being

careful to put no pressure on her swollen ankle, Nancy found Helene and Henri looking very serious.

Helene confessed that they were embarrassed about staying at the Drew home without being permitted to reimburse the lawyer.

"Oh, please stop thinking of that," said Nancy. "We just love having you here, and you can help me on the case as no one else could."

Henri brightened a little. "Nancy, I could do one thing that might help repay your kindness, but I'll need your cooperation."

He explained that he was a portrait painter as well as a dancer. His art was not well known, but he had done some acceptable work. He offered to paint Nancy's portrait as a reward for her help.

"Why, that would be wonderful!" said Nancy. "Dad has been trying for a long time to get me to have my portrait painted. He'll be thrilled."

"Then it's settled. As soon as we finish breakfast, we'll pick the right spot and I'll begin work."

Half an hour later they set up a studio in Hannah's second-floor sewing room. Nancy, wearing a dainty ice-blue blouse, sat quietly while Henri made several rough pencil sketches.

Finally he selected one that Helene declared looked exactly like Nancy.

"I like the expression, because it's serious and yet Nancy has a little smile," she said. "To me that is just the way she looks."

After she had posed for two hours, Nancy was glad to stretch a bit. She telephoned the dancing school and found that things were running smoothly.

Soon afterward, George arrived. "Hypers, Nancy!" she exclaimed. "I thought you'd be in bed. Where did you learn to fall down a whole flight of stairs and come up with nothing worse than a few bruises and a twisted ankle?"

"It takes a lot of practice," Nancy answered with a laugh.

"Anyway," said George, "I just dropped in to see if I could be your chauffeur."

"I certainly would like to go out and do some work on the case," Nancy replied. "Suppose you have lunch here and we'll start right afterward."

At two o'clock Nancy and George were on their way. Their first stop was the Civic Center, where George ran in to tell Mrs. Parsons that Nancy would be unable to rehearse for a few days.

"Now I'd like to cruise around," Nancy said, "on the off chance that I might see Mrs. Judson or that man who stopped me the other night."

Though George drove around for half an hour, the girls did not spot either of the people they sought. Next Nancy wanted to check hotel lobbies and restaurants.

"But you can't do that yourself," George objected, "and I don't know the man."

Nancy had an idea. "You go in, and if you find

anyone who seems to fit the description, I'll take a look."

George investigated hotels first, but saw no one who resembled either Mrs. Judson or the mysterious man. Next they tried a number of restaurants, where George looked over the clientele and asked cashiers and hat-check girls if anyone who ate there resembled the people they sought. All the replies were negative.

"Let's try one more," said Nancy late in the afternoon. George pulled up in front of a small dining place called the Regal Restaurant.

Both girls went inside. Nancy described the couple they wanted and told the cashier that the two would not necessarily have been together.

The woman thought for a few seconds, then said, "There was a couple in here last night that sounds like your description. The woman was an American. She was dressed in loud clothing and talked in a whiny voice. The man had a French accent."

"Did you overhear their names?" Nancy asked.

"The woman called the man Rowl—or something like that."

"Rowl?" Nancy repeated. "That might be Raoul. What were they talking about?"

The cashier thought for a moment. Then she said, "I didn't hear much. Apparently they were finishing a conversation they'd started before they got here. But the woman said, 'You'd better come across with a nice bit of jewelry for me or I'll spill the beans!' "

"That sounds like her!" said Nancy. "Do you remember anything else?"

"Only that the woman handed the man a letter when they were eating dessert."

At this point the cashier called to a waitress who had served the couple. The girl remembered them well.

"When the man read the letter," she said, "he looked plenty mad. And he gave the woman an awful scolding for losing the stamp."

"Have you any idea where they live?" Nancy asked.

The waitress said that she had heard them mention the big apartment house on Oakwood Avenue. "But I don't know that they live there."

Nancy thanked the cashier and the waitress, and the girls hurried off.

When they reached the apartment house, Nancy looked at every name on the letter boxes. Not one of them was Judson. She rang the superintendent's bell. There was no reply, but the front door opened and a woman came out. Nancy asked her whether a couple named Judson lived in the building. The woman said she did not know.

"Mr. Judson's a Frenchman," said Nancy with a smile. "Would that mean anything?"

"There's a Frenchman here. He lives in 1A."

The two girls walked down a corridor and knocked. The door was opened by a thin, sallow-cheeked man with a waxed mustache.

"Ah, *charmant!*" the Frenchman said. "The so pretty American girls."

The girls were amused by his exaggerated mannerisms. George asked, "Is there another Frenchman in this building who might be using the name of Judson?"

"I see you are not interested in poor Guion," said the man. "But yes, we have a Mr. and Mrs. Judson here for some weeks."

Nancy asked for a description of the couple. It sounded as though the woman was Mrs. Judson, and her husband might well be the man who had stopped her on the deserted road!

"Where are they living?" she asked.

Mr. Guion pointed down the corridor. "They have sublet down here, while the tenant is away in Canada. However," he said, shrugging, "I do not know where they are now. This morning they most quickly moved out."

CHAPTER VI

A Strange Mix-up

"To think we came so close to finding the Judsons and then missed them!" George fumed when she and Nancy were back in the convertible, heading for the Drew home.

Nancy, too, was discouraged, although it was interesting to know that she had been correct in suspecting that the man and woman who evidently had a major role in the Fontaine case had been living in River Heights.

"We could call the apartment superintendent to learn whether they left a forwarding address," the girl said. "But since they've been receiving mail at the General Post Office, that doesn't seem likely."

When George dropped Nancy at her home, Hannah Gruen greeted the young detective with a smile. "You have company!" she announced.

Nancy hobbled into the living room to find Ned Nickerson seated on the sofa.

"Hello!" he said. "Say, what's this I hear about a busted ankle?"

Nancy told him it was only a mild strain. "Then if you're okay," he said, "how about a double date tonight with the Fontaines?"

"All right. But we'll have to stay here," said Nancy. "It would be dangerous for them to leave the house. Won't you have dinner with us? I can promise apple pie."

"It's a deal."

The drapes were drawn throughout the first floor and the Fontaines came downstairs. Ned liked them at once, and they conversed freely.

During dinner Nancy told the group what she had learned at the Oakwood Avenue apartment house. Afterward, Mr. Drew excused himself and went to his study. The four young people sat in the living room and talked.

Suddenly the doorbell rang several times. The Fontaines looked worried and Nancy advised them to hide in the kitchen. As Helene and Henri hurried off, Hannah went to answer the bell.

Nancy and Ned watched from the living room while the housekeeper opened the door. They were amazed to see a man of medium build, his face concealed by a handkerchief he held in his hand, force his way in. He pushed past Hannah and shut the door behind him!

Ned ran into the hall, intending to tackle the intruder. The man stood still and whisked the handkerchief away from his face.

"What's the idea of forcing your way in here?" Ned demanded.

Nancy had hobbled to the hall and stood staring at the man in blank amazement. He was the one she had met on the plane—the person they suspected of having sent the warning note to the Fontaines!

He was thunderstruck when he recognized Nancy. "You live here?" he asked.

Before she could reply, there was a frantic pounding on the front door.

"Don't let anybody in!" the stranger cried. "I was followed!"

"Open the door!" cried a girl's voice, which Nancy recognized at once as George's.

Nancy opened the door and her friend rushed in. "Oh, I tried to warn you!" she exclaimed. "But this man—he got here ahead of me!"

"Warn them about what?" the stranger asked.

"About you," George said bluntly. "Nancy, get the police!"

"Police?" the man asked. "I don't know what this is all about. I didn't come here to cause any trouble."

"Then why are you here?" George demanded.

"I've come to see Mr. Carson Drew," the man answered. "I understand that he is an attorney. I have a case for him."

Mr. Drew had stepped out of his study when the commotion began. He now came forward. "I'm Carson Drew," he said. "And your name?"

"Johann Koff."

"Millie Koff's father?" Nancy exclaimed.

"Yes."

"I understood from Mrs. Parsons that you and Millie had left town and no one knew where you had gone," said Nancy.

Mr. Drew added, "You will forgive us if your mysterious disappearance seems suspicious to us?"

"I will explain everything," Mr. Koff said.

"You mean I've been shadowing you for nothing?" George exclaimed, sagging weakly against the door frame.

Mr. Koff laughed. For the first time he recognized George as the young woman who had demanded an interview of him the night before last.

"I assure you, the Drews do not need protection from me," the caller said. "Because I need your trust, I'd like to offer proof of my identity."

He took out a wallet and several letters, which he showed the lawyer. When Mr. Drew seemed satisfied with them, Mr. Koff added, "And now may we talk alone?"

Mr. Drew led the way into his study and closed the door. Nancy went to the kitchen and explained to the Fontaines what had happened. She advised that they remain there until Mr. Koff left the house.

Five minutes later Mr. Drew came to the door of the study and called to his daughter.

"Please come in, Nancy," he said. "I want you to hear an amazing story."

As Nancy seated herself in a chair alongside her father's desk, he told her that the caller was a writer for newspapers and magazines.

"I've come to your father," Koff explained, "with a law case that may also need a little detective work."

Mr. Koff leaned back in his chair, then went on, "I became excited on the plane, fearing it would crash, because I have much work to do for my native land of Centrovia, from which I escaped.

"I was so upset that I picked up a briefcase that I thought was my own. When I reached my hotel, I discovered that it belonged to someone else. The papers inside indicated that the owner was a Mr. Buzby in New York, so I sent the case to him, air mail, special delivery, at once.

"Then the trouble started. I received a phone call the following day from a man in River Heights who said that the briefcase belonged to him. Buzby had notified him and was sending it along. The man here is David Judson of Oakwood Avenue."

Nancy was startled to hear this name but felt it was best to reveal nothing at this time.

"This David Judson," the Centrovian went on, "told me that Mr. Buzby was a business competitor of his. As a result of seeing confidential material in the briefcase, he had learned business secrets and made a profit from them by getting several large orders. Mr. Judson claims he has suffered considerable financial loss because of it and is demanding damages from me."

"Could he collect?" Nancy asked her father.

"Under certain circumstances," the lawyer replied. "But listen to the rest of the story."

Koff continued, "Well, Judson was aggressive. He frightened me. My daughter and I packed at once and moved to the hotel in Cliffwood."

"But he found you?" Nancy asked.

"Yes, and tonight he made a new demand by phone. He said he had proof that I had deliberately taken his briefcase. A girl on the plane near me would swear to it."

Nancy was startled. Did Judson mean her? There had been no other girl sitting nearby.

"If he produces this witness," said Nancy firmly, "she'll be a phony. Don't worry about that."

"I feel that the whole thing is a frame-up," Mr. Drew stated. "This Judson hopes to get some money easily. We'll try to put a stop to the threats at once. Suppose you drop a note to Mr. Judson, telling him that you have turned the matter over to me. If he still wishes to bring suit against you, I'll agree to accept the case."

"But I understand through a friend who spoke to the superintendent that Mr. Judson has left Oakwood Avenue and did not say where he was going," Koff objected.

"You might try General Delivery at the post office," Nancy suggested.

"I will do that," the Centrovian agreed.

Mr. Drew asked, "Did you get your briefcase back?"

"No. Mr. Buzby wrote that he knew nothing about mine. It contained both my name and address but has not been returned." Koff's face grew grim. "There are many valuable things in it and I am concerned that the information may fall into the wrong hands."

"The wrong hands?" Nancy repeated.

"In my briefcase," he explained, "were a number of letters from the Centrovian underground in various countries. Through them, the occupying authorities might trace the loyal people who are working for us. I am sick with worry."

Nancy felt sorry for Koff. "I hope everything will soon be straightened out," she said, "and that your daughter can return to the charity show. I understand she's a wonderful dancer."

"Yes," Koff agreed, relaxing a moment. Then his voice rose excitedly. "Before the occupation there were many wonderful dancers in Centrovia. But no more. No, no more. The hearts of our people are crushed. They do not have the time or the spirit for singing and dancing."

"Did you know many of the famous Centrovian dancers?" Nancy asked.

"Indeed I did," Koff replied. "Most were killed, but a few fled the country at the time I did. I remember one family in particular, the Provaks, who went to Paris. The mother, an exquisite beauty, died there, and her husband did too. I learned from the underground that the children might be in grave danger."

"What are their names?"

"They're known as Helene and Henri Fontaine."

Nancy heard his words with mixed feelings. Her old suspicion that Koff might be playing a double role flashed across her mind.

The young sleuth glanced at her father's puzzled face. Evidently he, too, was trying to decide whether they ought to call in the Fontaines.

Catching Nancy's eye, Carson Drew shook his head slowly as if to say, "Give nothing away!"

But the decision not to reveal the whereabouts of their guests was suddenly taken from them. Helene and Henri Fontaine hurried into the room!

CHAPTER VII

Masked Intruders

FOR the next few minutes there was near pandemonium in Mr. Drew's study. Mr. Koff and the Fontaines were speaking Centrovian at the tops of their voices, their eyes flashing and hands waving.

As Nancy and her father stood by helplessly, Ned Nickerson, Hannah, and George rushed in. "I knew there'd be trouble! I just knew it!" Hannah cried.

By the sound of the Centrovians' excited voices, the onlookers fully expected Koff and Henri to come to blows. To their amazement, nothing of the sort happened. But when Mr. Drew caught the word Judson, he stepped forward and took Henri by the shoulder.

"Please speak English," he said.

The young man looked embarrassed. He bowed slightly and said, "I beg your pardon, sir. We

Centrovians are excitable people. We were saying nothing you should not hear."

The interruption quieted the three Centrovians. Helene and Mr. Koff also apologized, explaining that they were talking about conditions in Centrovia. Henri had also mentioned Nancy's suspicions about the Judsons.

Helene and Henri, who had overheard part of their countryman's conversation with the Drews, had not been able to remain in hiding when they heard Mr. Koff mention their names.

Nancy addressed herself to the Fontaines. She asked them frankly, "Do you want to tell Mr. Koff your whole story?"

"Oh, yes," Henri replied.

From an inside pocket of his jacket he pulled out the warning note that had been left at the dancing school and showed it to the caller. After reading it, Mr. Koff remarked, "This just proves what I have been telling the Provaks—they are in danger."

"We thought you sent that note!" George blurted out.

"Me!" Koff exclaimed. Then he smiled at George. "Is that why you've been following me?"

She admitted that it was.

"Well, I'm glad we're getting things straightened out," said Koff. "And now I must go." He turned to Mr. Drew. "You will take my case against Mr. Judson?"

The lawyer nodded, then said, "Since I am handling your case, there are a few things I would like you to do. For one, everything that took place in this house tonight must be kept in strictest confidence."

Koff nodded.

"Also," Mr. Drew went on, "I see no reason for your hiding. If you wish to move back to the Claymore Hotel, I think it will simplify matters. It might bring Mr. Judson into the open, and I should like very much to meet him."

"My daughter and I will come back to River Heights tomorrow," Mr. Koff promised. "I know Millie will be pleased. She can resume her part in the charity performance."

Nancy smiled. "Mrs. Parsons will be glad to hear it. I'll tell her."

The Centrovian said good night and left the house. The others sat down to discuss this newest development.

"I just can't make up my mind about that man," George said flatly. "One minute I trust him and the next I don't."

The Fontaines were confused by this observation. They trusted the man implicitly.

Mr. Drew and Nancy said that they felt a bit wary about Mr. Koff. Undercover agents were very clever. Helene and Henri admitted that perhaps they had told him too much.

"Oh, what shall we do?" Helene cried nervously.

Nancy had a ready answer. "I believe we should move you to another place."

"We'll go," said Henri. "But where? We seem to cause trouble for ourselves and everyone else wherever we are."

At this point Ned spoke. "I know the ideal spot for you. None of your enemies would ever think of it. My family owns a little place on Cedar Lake that they're not using right now. I'm sure my parents would be glad to have you live there."

"That's an excellent idea," Nancy declared. "Ned, find out about it right away, will you?"

He telephoned his mother at once. When Ned explained the situation, Mrs. Nickerson said she would be very happy to have the Fontaines use the cottage.

"It's all settled," he announced, coming back to the group. "When would you like to go?"

Nancy answered the question by saying she thought the Fontaines should leave immediately. She suggested that they pack while she and Hannah filled some cartons with food for them to take along.

Secretly Nancy and George were amused at Hannah's reaction to the whole episode. She seemed delighted to have her guests leave and, with Nancy's help, packed a large quantity of food.

Ned pulled his car into the driveway and parked near the back door. Suitcases and cartons were stowed in the trunk; then the Fontaines stepped into the rear seat and crouched down. Ned and Nancy climbed into the front.

As soon as they had gone, Mr. Drew got out his car and drove George home. He had just returned and was taking off his coat when the telephone rang. Hannah, on her way to the living room, heard him say, "I'll be there as soon as I can make it."

As he replaced the receiver, Hannah said, "Are you going out?"

"Yes, Hannah. The call was from Mr. Koff. He has a lead in connection with his case and is going to New York. He is leaving now and I'm to meet him there. I'll take the next flight in about an hour."

After the lawyer had left the house, Hannah sat down in the living room to read. Ten minutes later, she heard footsteps on the front porch.

"Nancy and Ned," she thought. "Oh, dear, something must have happened and they couldn't continue to the lake."

Knowing that Nancy had a key, Hannah did not get up. But a moment later, when the bell rang, she thought that Nancy must have forgotten her key.

"Well, I can't blame her with all the things she has on her mind," the housekeeper said to herself. She rose and walked to the door.

As she opened it, Hannah Gruen froze to the spot. A man and woman wearing masks stood there! They rushed inside, slammed the door shut, and the man said gruffly with a French accent, "There is nothing to fear if you will do as we say. Where are the Fontaines?"

Hannah shuddered. Then she gained control of herself and said bravely, "You're making a serious mistake. This is the Drew residence. There's no one here by the name of Fontaine."

"We happen to know they are here," the woman declared. She spoke without accent and in a nasal tone.

At this moment there was an unexpected interruption. Togo, Nancy's terrier, rushed in from the kitchen and leaped at the man. In a lightning-like move the masked stranger threw the dog to the floor, pulled a drape from the hall window, and quickly wrapped the terrier in it.

Hannah sprang into action. "Get out of here! Both of you!" she shouted, moving backward toward the telephone.

The intruders apparently guessed what was in the housekeeper's mind. Roughly the man grabbed her by the shoulders and pushed her into the living room. He glanced around, then said to his companion, "Go find some rope!"

The woman disappeared toward the kitchen. Hannah could hear her opening and slamming drawers. Finally she came back with a roll of clothesline.

Quickly, Hannah was bound to a chair. Then the couple disappeared up the stairway. Apparently they were making a thorough search of the residence, because Hannah heard them going to the third floor.

Satisfied that the Fontaines were not hiding at the Drew residence, the masked strangers stormed down the stairs. The man entered the living room and stood before Hannah Gruen. Glaring at her and shaking his fist, he cried out, "You tell us where Helene and Henri Fontaine are, or you'll regret it for the rest of your life!"

CHAPTER VIII

The Artist's Knife

As the Fontaines left the Drew home with Nancy and Ned, they felt relieved. They talked about the lighter side of their lives in France and described amusing incidents in connection with their dancing. Nancy was delighted.

Later, they approached the Nickersons' cottage on the shore of Cedar Lake. Helene said cheerfully, "This is a charming spot. I am sure my brother and I will enjoy staying here."

Ned said he hoped so; then a grim expression crossed his face. The cabin, now visible among the trees, had a dim light in it!

Nancy saw the light too. "Someone's here," she said tensely to Ned. "That's strange. But how could anybody possibly have known that we were coming?"

"Maybe a tramp has broken in," Ned replied calmly. "I'll go and investigate. You wait here."

Bent low, he sneaked up to the cabin. Then straightening up a little, he peered through one of the windows. Almost immediately he came hurrying back to the car, laughing heartily. He said, "Nancy, you'll never believe who's here."

"Who?" Nancy asked.

"Nobody dangerous. Just a couple of my fraternity brothers. They have a standing invitation to use the place whenever they want to."

Not understanding such a custom, the Fontaines were afraid they would be considered intruders.

"We will not stay. We do not want to spoil the fun of your brothers," Helene demurred.

It took several minutes of persuasion to convince the Fontaines everything would be all right.

"There's no reason why all of you can't stay here together," Ned insisted. "You can depend upon the boys to keep your secret. In fact, it might be a good thing to have a couple of strong-armed guys on hand if any of your enemies show up."

Helene laughed. "I have heard much about these American fraternity boys. It will be nice to meet some of them."

"And will they be glad to meet you!" Ned said.

He went inside the cabin to explain the arrangement to his friends while Henri and the girls unloaded the car. Presently two good-looking youths, one tall and blond, the other short and dark, strode down the path.

"Hi, Nancy!" said the tall one.

"Hello, Steve," she answered, and to the shorter boy, "Art, how are you?"

The Fontaines were introduced and at once both boys became very solicitous about Helene. Conversing gaily, they escorted her toward the cabin. Nancy followed, with Ned and Henri carrying the luggage. The young detective smiled. The plan was working out even better than she had anticipated! The various angles of the mystery were explained to Steve and Art.

At the end Nancy remarked, "As you can see, this whole business has to be kept secret. The lives of the Fontaines may be in danger if anyone finds out where they are."

Steve said, "You can count on us for protection —at least until late tomorrow night. Then we'll have to leave."

Nancy turned to the brother and sister. "I'll be out to see you. In the meantime, we can keep in touch with one another by phone. I suggest we don't use names, though. Let's identify ourselves with the word *scarlet*."

"Good," Helene agreed. Then impulsively she threw her arms around Nancy's neck and kissed her.

Steve whistled. "Wish I were a detective," he said, and Helene blushed.

Henri thanked Nancy and Ned for coming to the Fontaines' rescue and wished them a safe trip home.

The young detective and her date drove back to River Heights silently for a while; then Ned chuckled. "It isn't often that I get a chance to ride along the Muskoka River with you in the moonlight. Guess I can thank my lucky stars tonight."

Nancy smiled and looked up at the sky. The conversation continued in a light vein until they pulled up in front of the Drew home and walked to the door. Then Nancy again became the alert investigator. The house was dark and she heard Togo barking furiously.

"Something must be wrong, Ned. Dad and Hannah would never allow Togo to keep barking. And there's always a light on."

Nancy unlocked the door and she and Ned stepped into the hallway. Ned clicked on the light. The dog was not in sight and the barking seemed curiously muffled.

"Togo's in the coat closet," said Ned, going toward a door under the stairway.

At the same time, Nancy caught a glimpse of the Drews' housekeeper gagged and tied to a chair in the living room. Quickly the young detective snapped on a light and hurried over to the woman.

"Hannah!" Nancy cried, aghast, removing the gag. "Who did this? The fiend!"

At first Mrs. Gruen could not even speak, but she took several deep breaths as Nancy untied the

"Hannah!" Nancy cried. *"Who did this to you?"*

bonds and slipped them off. Nancy's outburst had brought Ned from the hall, a whimpering Togo in his arms. He stared in astonishment.

Finally Mrs. Gruen said, "He was a fiend all right. She was too. But I didn't tell them! I didn't! I didn't say a word!"

"Who?" Ned asked in bewilderment.

Nancy realized that the woman was hysterical. Hannah got only as far as explaining where Mr. Drew had gone, then had to give up. Nancy put an arm around her.

"Hannah, dear, you've had an awful fright and I want to know what happened. But don't try to talk any more until you rest and I bring you some tea."

As she started for the kitchen, Togo leaped from Ned's arms into Nancy's and began licking her in overjoyed affection. She carried him with her and gave him a puppy biscuit.

Nancy returned to the living room in a few minutes with tea. Between sips, Hannah, somewhat recovered, told her story.

"Brave little Togo," she said in conclusion. "I guess he's the reason that awful man didn't carry out his threat to harm me. Togo got out of the drapery he'd been rolled in and nearly bit the woman. Then the man forced the dog into the closet. But Togo kept barking so loudly, he frightened the couple away."

Nancy hugged her pet. "Togo, you've really done a wonderful job tonight."

Hannah Gruen was more composed now and gave Nancy a description of the intruders.

"That sounds like the Judsons," Nancy commented. "Ned, let's look around and see if by chance they left any clues."

First she helped Hannah to her room; then she and Ned turned on all the lights in the house and began to check the dwelling from cellar to attic. So far as clues were concerned, it looked for a while as though the search was to be futile.

But while the couple were in the attic, Nancy leaned over a trunk near one corner and spotted a small object on the floor behind it. In the light she saw that it was a knife. Since it did not belong to the Drews, the Judsons must have dropped it.

"I think it's a palette knife used by artists for mixing paints," Nancy commented. "It probably dropped out of one of Mr. Judson's pockets when he bent over to look behind the trunk."

The knife was a simple one with a polished wooden handle. Near the base of it had been carved a small R. For Raoul? Nancy speculated.

"Does this mean that Mr. Judson is an artist?" Ned asked.

"I wonder," Nancy speculated.

CHAPTER IX

Ballet Interlude

FOR nearly an hour Nancy and Ned talked about the possible meaning of the R on the artist's palette knife. Both were sure it had special significance.

"Have you any idea how you might find out more about it?" Ned asked.

"I think I'll go over to that apartment house on Oakwood Avenue tomorrow and interview the superintendent and that Frenchman who knew the Judsons."

"I'll go along," said Ned with a wink. "Bess told me about Monsieur Guion."

Nancy laughed, assuring Ned that the man did not interest her. She said she would be delighted to have Ned go along.

Early the next afternoon, a beautiful Sunday with a brilliant blue sky, Ned picked Nancy up in his car and they drove to Oakwood Avenue. As before, the superintendent did not answer his bell, so Nancy pressed the one for the Guion apartment.

The inner door of the apartment house opened quickly, and Nancy and Ned walked down to 1A. The Frenchman stood in the doorway.

"Ah, you have come back, mademoiselle," he said with a smile. "And you have brought your fiancé?"

As he spoke, Monsieur Guion twirled one end of his mustache and invited the couple in. They followed him and sat down.

"You were a great help to me the other day when you answered my questions about the Judsons," said Nancy. "I'd like to ask you some more."

"Your wish is my command," Guion replied with a sweeping bow.

Ned frowned but said nothing. Nancy asked the Frenchman if Mr. Judson was an artist.

"Oh, no!" Guion said, shaking his head vigorously.

"Does he have any friends who are artists?" the young detective asked.

"That I do not know," Guion answered. "We did not become good friends. He is what you Americans call a washout. He was not good company. I did not like him."

"You have been very kind," Nancy said after a while, rising. Then she and Ned left. When they reached the Drew residence, Nancy was pleased to learn that her father had arrived. She asked him about the outcome of his trip to New York.

The lawyer's face clouded. "It was a wild-goose chase! A hoax!"

Nancy and Ned were amazed. "You mean Mr. Koff didn't meet you?" Nancy asked.

"He not only didn't meet me, but swore that he had never sent the message," Mr. Drew replied. "I waited a long time at the New York Airport, then telephoned Mr. Koff at the Cliffwood Hotel. He was astonished to hear what had happened."

"But his voice?" Nancy suggested to her father.

"Whoever called me," said Mr. Drew angrily, "imitated Johann Koff's voice perfectly. But I can't understand why I was tricked."

His daughter told him what had happened at the house the previous evening, and Hannah, who had entered the room, gave her version of the story.

"Someone wanted me out of the way," the lawyer said. "I can't understand why I was sent so far away, though."

"Unless a person connected with the Fontaine case was in New York and followed you to see where you would go. Where did you spend the night?" Nancy asked.

"At your Aunt Eloise's," her father answered. "We went to church this morning and had dinner before I left. I hope she won't become involved in this."

Mr. Drew now asked what his daughter had been doing during his absence. She showed him the knife with the R on it. He examined it carefully but could not explain why a man who was not an artist should be carrying it.

"Perhaps Henri might know a reason," he suggested.

Nancy telephoned him. When the young man answered, she said, "Scarlet."

"Scarlet here," was the reply.

Nancy told him about the knife in guarded tones, knowing the Cedar Lake phone was a party line, but Henri could not explain why anyone but an artist would use a palette knife.

"This puzzle is too much for me," said Ned, rising. "Let's take a walk, Nancy."

She suggested that they call on Mrs. Parsons to tell her Millie Koff was returning to the charity show. The woman was delighted to hear the good news.

"But, my dear," she said, "this doesn't mean we're going to lose you! No, indeed, you're going to stay in the show."

"I don't understand, Mrs. Parsons," Nancy answered.

Mrs. Parsons said that Millie Koff would still dance in the performance. But another soloist had dropped out.

"So you can do your dance in place of hers."
The woman chuckled.

Nancy tried to beg off, but Mrs. Parsons took
both of the girl's hands in her own. "Please," she
begged, "take the part. You danced so beautifully
the other day we *must* have you in the show."

Ned urged her to do so, and Nancy finally accepted. She said she expected her ankle to be all
right in a couple of days and would then come to
rehearsals.

The following morning Nancy received a
phone call from Mrs. Nickerson. Ned's mother
explained that due to the illness of a close friend
who needed her help, she could not go to the
dancing school that day. Nancy promised to take
her place as receptionist.

Bess arrived at about two o'clock, looking
flustered and worried. Nancy asked what the trouble was.

"Oh, I haven't had one minute to look up anything about the history of the dance," she said.
"Nancy, you'll just have to do that part for me."

Nancy said she would be happy to do it. Bess
insisted that Nancy put on a ballet costume, so
that she would look the part. To please her, the
young detective did so.

The first group of ballet students were very
attentive to both the story and the dance lesson,
and the two girls were delighted with their prog-

ress. As a younger group came in, Bess whispered that she was simply famished.

"Nancy," she said, "be a darling and keep talking to those girls while I run out for a soda."

"But how about the calorie count?" Nancy reminded the plump girl with a laugh.

"Oh, just one soda won't make any difference," Bess insisted. She slipped a coat over her dancing costume and went down the stairway.

Nancy helped the children into their leotards, then went into the practice room with them. They sat in a semicircle on the floor, with Nancy on a bench facing them.

"Ballet is a very old dance form," she began. "Classical ballet tells a story—happy, or sad, or exciting without the use of words. Nowadays we still tell stories or express emotions by dancing to appropriate music.

"The great ballet artists know just what movements of the dance go with various types of music. Today let's concentrate on interpretative dance. Susie," said Nancy to a blue-eyed child, "I'll put on a record and you dance whatever you think it might represent."

Nancy started the "Parade of the Wooden Soldiers." Instantly Susie marched, stiff-legged, around the room.

"Good!" said Nancy. "And now, Carol, here's one for you."

Carol listened and pretended to be walking with her doll.

"That's right." Nancy smiled. "This is the 'Waltzing Doll.' As you become acquainted with more difficult music, steps to go with it will come to you at once. All you learn now are the different kinds of steps and movements. Later, when you are told the story of a ballet, you will interpret it in your own way."

"You mean this lesson we can do any steps we want to the music? Oh, let's all try one right now," begged black-haired Jennifer.

"All right," Nancy agreed. She told a story of an animal parade and dropped "Forest Frolic" over the pin of the turntable.

The little girls rose, listened a moment, then started to dance, imitating both the movements and cries of various animals of the forest. A lion roared and stalked a leaping deer. A bear growled, monkeys chattered, and a wild dog barked.

In the midst of the din, Susie suddenly stopped dancing and screamed. She pointed toward the reception room and cried out, "Look! There's a witch out there!"

Nancy turned to see a strange sight. A woman, wearing a tight-fitting black dress and large peaked hat, with a stole covering half of her face, was tiptoeing across the carpeted room toward the desk.

"Look! There's a witch!" Susie screamed.

For a moment, Nancy could not understand her strange actions. There was nothing in the desk she could possibly want. Suddenly, in spite of the woman's disguise, Nancy recognized her. "Mrs. Judson!" she called out involuntarily.

Realizing she had been discovered, the woman forgot her attempts at stealth, ran forward boldly, and reached up on the wall. When her hand came down, she was holding the scarlet slippers!

"Drop those at once!" Nancy shouted, running into the reception room.

But Mrs. Judson, clutching the ballet shoes against her chest, rushed to the hall and down the stairs. Nancy raced across the reception room after the thief!

CHAPTER X

Quest for Portraits

As Nancy dashed out the front door after the thief, she saw Bess heading for the dancing school.

"Hurry! Watch the children! I have to catch a thief!"

Nancy's ankle was still painful and Mrs. Judson outdistanced her, disappearing around the next corner. Nancy looked for her in vain and concluded she had gone through one of the stores to another street.

As Nancy paused, she realized that her scanty ballet outfit was attracting stares on the busy street. She blushed and quickly walked back to the dancing school. Her young pupils were trying to explain to Bess about the "witch" who had taken the slippers. When they saw Nancy, they all asked what had happened.

"I didn't catch the woman," she said.

"Miss Fontaine will feel bad," Susie said. "She just loves those slippers."

Bess led the children into the practice room and continued their lesson. Nancy, meanwhile, telephoned the police about the theft.

"There must be something significant about the ballet slippers to make Mrs. Judson steal them," she thought. "But what?" She decided to drive out to ask the Fontaines about the shoes.

She got in touch with George, who promised to relieve her as receptionist at the school.

When Nancy reached home, her father was already there. He readily agreed to accompany her to Cedar Lake.

"I learned a few things today that the Fontaines may be able to shed some light on," he said. "I talked with the airline stewardess who was on that plane you and Koff took. She told me one of the passengers spoke with a decided French accent, though his name wasn't French. He was listed as Raymond Bull. Furthermore, he too got off the plane at River Heights."

Nancy thought of the letter R on the palette knife. Could Raymond Bull be an artist friend of the Judsons?

"Then," Mr. Drew went on, "I phoned all the hotels in town. But no one named Raymond Bull was registered at any of them. It's probably an assumed name."

When the Drews arrived at the Nickerson lodge

two hours later, they found the Fontaines seated in rocking chairs on the front porch. Regretfully, Nancy told them of the unpleasant incident at the dancing school that afternoon.

"Oh, my darling slippers!" Helene exclaimed. Tears sprang to her eyes.

"I'm sure we'll get them back," said Nancy. "But have you any idea why Mrs. Judson stole your mother's ballet slippers?"

"No. None."

"Do they have any special value besides the sentimental one?"

Henri leaned forward. "They may have," he answered. "The slippers appeared in a portrait that has a curious story."

"Please tell me," Nancy urged.

"Nearly two years ago," Henri began, "while I was still painting portraits, a man by the name of Tomas Renee came to me. He ordered twelve pictures of a dancer in various ballet poses. It took me six months to complete the paintings."

"And the slippers?" Nancy prompted.

"Helene posed for me, and in the last picture she wore the scarlet slippers. In the others she wore her own pink ones."

"Monsieur Renee's name begins with an R," Nancy observed. "May he be considered a possible owner of the palette knife?"

"I suppose so," said Henri, "except that he was an art dealer, not a painter, so far as I know.

Well, the first strange thing was that Monsieur Renee put a peculiar paragraph in our contract— the whole transaction was to be kept secret and I was not to sign the paintings."

"That was odd," Nancy murmured.

"He said that there was a race among dealers to fill an order from a famous dancing school for twelve paintings. Monsieur Renee wanted no one to know that he was entering this race."

Henri went on to say that Renee's wife fancied herself to be a great ballet dancer and wished to model for the portraits.

"When this Madame Renee came to my studio, I found that she was a miserable dancer. And she could not pose in any of the positions for more than a few seconds.

"Finally I had to tell Monsieur Renee this. He insisted that we must complete the paintings, and permitted my sister to be the model."

"But Madame Renee was very jealous," Helene put in.

"Yes," said Henri. "She claimed that her husband's visits to our studio were only for the purpose of seeing Helene. And just as I was finishing the last picture, the warning note came, telling Helene and me to leave the country."

"Do you think Renee could have had anything to do with the note?" Nancy asked.

"I didn't at the time," Henri replied. "But now I think it's possible."

The young detective turned to her father. "Dad, do you think you could find out more about Tomas Renee?"

"It may take time," the lawyer replied. "But my attorney friend, Mr. Scott, happens to be in Paris at the moment. I'll cable and ask him to track down this new suspect."

"And now," Henri said, "I have an opportunity to continue work on Nancy's portrait!"

Mr. Drew said he was not in a hurry to return to River Heights. While Henri prepared to work, the lawyer wrote out his cable and used the lodge telephone to send it to Mr. Scott.

When the Drews said good night much later, both were pleased with the progress on the portrait, which Mr. Drew declared was to be his Christmas present.

The following morning Nancy found that Hannah did not feel well. She suggested that the housekeeper let her take over for a while.

As she did the household chores, the girl detective tried to fit the pieces of the Fontaine puzzle together. Three R's: Raoul Judson, Raymond Bull, Tomas Renee. Were they associates? Were the names aliases? And what did the strange number in the figurine and on the stamp of the Parisian letter mean?

She was interrupted by the telephone. It was Mr. Drew, calling from his office.

"I have some interesting news for you," he

said, "but I'd rather not give it to you over the telephone. I suggest you come down here at once."

Nancy lost no time in getting to her father's office. He closed the door as she sat down in his private study.

"What is it?" Nancy asked eagerly.

"Tomas Renee has disappeared. And he's wanted by the French police!"

Mr. Drew explained that up to six months before, the Renees had lived in a villa outside Paris. Then suddenly they had vanished.

"But," said the lawyer, "it seems that Mr. Renee had some strange dealings with various people and is liable to imprisonment."

"No wonder he disappeared," said Nancy. "I wonder if he is still in France."

"That's hard to say," her father answered. "If he left the country, it must have been under an assumed name."

"Then the immigration authorities can't help us?"

"I've spoken with them," said Mr. Drew. "If Tomas Renee came to the United States, it was not under the names of Renee, Judson, or Bull. No one from France has arrived under those names during the past year and a half."

Nancy sighed. "All our facts are on the negative side, Dad. Let's try a new angle."

"What?"

"Those pictures that Henri painted may be an important clue," Nancy pointed out. "If Renee was dishonest, his story about the race among art dealers probably was false. And in the light of what's been happening to the Fontaines, there's a chance that some of the pictures may be in this country—possibly even in River Heights!"

"You think there is some connection between the paintings and the enemies of the Centrovian underground?"

"Perhaps."

Mr. Drew looked thoughtful. "Suppose I call the customs office? And then, how about having lunch with me?"

"Wonderful, Dad. I'll call Hannah and tell her I won't be home."

Nancy spoke to the housekeeper on a phone in the outer office, while Mr. Drew used his private line to call customs.

"Oh, Nancy," Hannah said, "I'm glad you called. Mrs. Parsons was here. She's terribly upset because Millie Koff didn't come back. She says the Koffs haven't returned to the Claymore Hotel."

Nancy hung up and dialed the Cliffwood Hotel at once. "Mr. Koff and his daughter checked out yesterday," the clerk told her. "They left no forwarding address."

Nancy was dumfounded. Had she let Mr. Koff deceive her? Was he in league with the Judsons, and maybe with Raymond Bull, and even Renee?

When Nancy told her father about the Koffs, the lawyer looked grave. "Let's eat," he suggested. "Maybe we'll be brighter after lunch and can figure this out."

At the lawyer's club, Nancy found herself the center of attention. Her father's friends enjoyed exchanging sallies with the young detective and trying to stump her on knotty problems. For a time, Nancy nearly forgot her own case.

Soon after they returned to Mr. Drew's office, a call came in from the customs office. Mr. Drew told Nancy that all of Henri's paintings had been shipped to the United States during the past twelve months.

"The consignor for eleven of them was Tomas Renee. But the twelfth, the one with the scarlet slippers, was sent over by a man signing the name Raoul Amien."

"Who received them in the United States?" Nancy asked eagerly.

"A Pierre Duparc, formerly an art dealer in New York. His whereabouts are unknown."

Nancy had a hunch. "Dad, I think this Raoul Amien may be in our vicinity—perhaps using the name Judson. Can we send a cable to Paris to inquire about him?"

Carson Drew agreed to do so, and Nancy said he would be able to reach her at the dancing school all afternoon.

When the lawyer returned home that evening, he told his daughter that Raoul Amien had indeed come to the United States. "He married after arriving," he added.

"Dad, I think Amien and Renee probably were working some scheme together—something to do with Henri's paintings." Nancy speculated. "It's even possible that they're enemies and the Fontaines are in the middle."

The lawyer laughed, pleased at his daughter's knack for quick deductions. "So what's your next move?"

"I think I'll go down and place an ad in the *Gazette* for a painting of a ballet dancer. Maybe I can locate some of Henri's work. Dad, please tell Hannah I'll be back in time for dinner."

The next morning Nancy's advertisement appeared in the local newspaper. She called Bess and George and asked them to come to her home as soon as possible.

"We'll go to the *Gazette* office at about three," she told the cousins a short time later. "I have a hunch that one of the suspects may mail or send a note and come to see who put the ad in the paper. I'd like you two to keep an eye on anyone who may be standing around when I go in to pick up the mail. See whether anyone seems particularly interested."

That afternoon Nancy drove downtown, parked near the entrance of the *Gazette,* and strolled in.

Her two friends were waiting at vantage points near the large pillars inside the building.

Nancy handed in the receipt for her box number and received three letters. Suddenly Bess signaled frantically and pointed out the window.

Johann Koff was watching Nancy intently!

Nancy stuffed the three letters into her handbag and went outside. Mr. Koff had not moved. Before she could speak, he smiled pleasantly.

"How are you?" he asked. "I just happened to see you crossing the street, and waited to speak to you."

The man explained that he and Millie had just returned to the Claymore after stopping overnight on the way back from the Cliffwood. He wondered whether there was any news on his case.

Nancy, taken aback, could not feel sure about the man. "Have you received any more threatening messages from Mr. Judson?" she asked.

"No. Perhaps that letter I sent about retaining your father on the case reached Mr. Judson and discouraged him from suing me."

Nancy, still slightly suspicious, asked, "Are Renee and Amien friends of yours?"

"I never heard of them." Suddenly Mr. Koff laughed. "Miss Detective, were you trying to trap me? Are these men enemies of the Centrovian underground?"

As Nancy merely smiled and did not reply, he

added, "I have heard nothing concerning my own briefcase. I am terribly worried."

"I wish I could help locate it," Nancy said. "And I'll tell Dad I saw you."

Joining her friends in the car, Nancy learned that no other suspicious characters had been spotted in the *Gazette* building. The young detective asked Bess to take the wheel so she could read the answers to the ad.

As they drove off, Nancy laid two of the letters on her lap. She opened the third. As she spread the sheet, both she and George gasped in astonishment.

"What is it?" Bess demanded, stopping for a traffic light.

Nancy held up the paper for her to read. On it had been sketched the familiar scarlet slipper insigne. In printed letters, similar to those on the note received by the Fontaines, were the words:

STOP YOUR DETECTIVE WORK AT ONCE OR YOU WILL FIND YOURSELF IN GRAVE PERIL!

CHAPTER XI

Signs of Tampering

BESS did not pull ahead when the traffic light turned green. She was too shaken by the threatening message Nancy had just received.

Horns began to sound and George urged, "Move, Bess!"

Bess drove on, then said worriedly, "Whoever wrote that note means business, Nancy. Oh, please give up the case before you run into real trouble."

"This doesn't scare me," Nancy declared. "Writers of anonymous notes are always cowards, and I don't intend to be frightened by one!"

Bess turned to George for moral support, but her cousin agreed with Nancy. She suggested that her friend open the other two notes.

"Oh, I hope they're not the same kind!" Bess said fearfully.

Nancy quickly examined the two answers and reassured her friends. One letter offered a painting that obviously was not one of the group Henri had painted. But the other note, which had been telephoned in, looked like a lead.

It was from the Elite Dancing School in Stanford, and described an oil painting the school was willing to sell. It depicted a ballet dancer in pink-and-white tulle, with an indistinct background of trees.

"That's just the way Henri described the background to me," said Nancy excitedly.

"Let's go right over to Stanford and look at it!" George urged.

"But we can't do that," Bess broke in. "Nancy and I have classes at the dancing school."

"Bess is right," said Nancy. "We'll go tomorrow morning."

When the girls arrived at the school, George left the others, arranging to meet them at nine the next day.

Bess had the first group of young ballerinas, Nancy the second. Both girls carried on with their usual enthusiasm but were surprised at the small attendance in the classes. More than half the pupils were absent.

"This is very strange," Nancy thought. "I wonder what the trouble is."

She made a list of the absentees and began telephoning their parents. Nancy explained to those she reached that she was sure the Fontaines would return soon to resume teaching.

In her conversations with the various mothers, Nancy noticed a reluctance to discuss the subject. Finally she talked to Mrs. Muller, a neighbor, and asked, "Has anyone been in touch with you regarding the Fontaines?"

"How did you know?" the woman said in surprise.

"Maybe it's my instinct," Nancy replied with a chuckle. "Just what have you heard?"

Mrs. Muller told her that several mothers, including her, had received anonymous letters informing them that the Fontaines had disappeared because they were wanted by the police. The letters indicated that the dancers were involved in a serious scandal, which would reflect on the children if they continued at the school.

"How wicked!" Nancy exclaimed. "Mrs. Muller, there isn't one word of truth in that story!"

"How can you be sure?" the woman asked.

"Because my father is handling the affairs of the Fontaines and knows all about their dealings. I'm sure you realize that I wouldn't be involved with them if anything dishonest were going on. My friends and I have worked hard to keep the school running, and naturally our success depends upon the cooperation of the parents. Won't you please allow your little girl to continue her lessons?"

Mrs. Muller finally agreed to send her child back. She suggested that Nancy call the other mothers and reassure them there was no truth to the letters. Nancy got busy on the telephone at once, explaining the situation to the women. They promised to allow their children to continue dancing lessons.

"Well, that's cleared up," Nancy said to Bess with a sigh of relief as she finished talking to the last person on the list. "They'll go along with the present arrangement."

"Thank goodness!" Bess said. But in a whisper she added, "Nancy, do you think there might be any basis for the idea that the Fontaines are wanted by the authorities?"

"I can't believe it," Nancy insisted. "And besides, I wouldn't take the word of anyone who is afraid to sign his name to a letter."

"Nor I," said Bess stoutly.

The next morning, she and George arrived at Nancy's house, and the three girls set off in the convertible. They reached Stanford a little after eleven o'clock and had no difficulty finding the Elite Dancing School.

Nancy went in alone and identified herself as the advertiser in the *Gazette*. The owner, Mr. Harlan, brought out the painting of the ballet dancer.

It was indeed a portrait of Helene and she was wearing the scarlet slippers!

"I bought this picture about six months ago," Mr. Harlan told Nancy. "It's very pleasing, but I'm remodeling and will have no room for it. I'd be willing to sell it to you for a small profit."

Trying hard not to show her elation, she asked the price.

"Thirty-five dollars," the Elite owner replied.

"I'll buy the picture," Nancy said. She opened her purse and paid him.

Nancy recalled the price Renee had paid Henri for the work. It was many times that amount. She was curious about the person from whom Mr. Harlan had bought the painting.

"Would you mind telling me who sold you the painting?" she asked.

"Not at all, but six months is a long time to remember details. A man with reddish hair came into the school and offered me the picture. The price was right, so I bought it."

Reddish hair, Nancy thought. This did not fit Judson or Warte, who had fraudulently sold the bisque dolls, or Renee, but one of them might have been wearing a wig!

"Did the man have a foreign accent?" she said. "And did he give his name?"

"No," Mr. Harlan answered to both questions. "Is something the matter with the painting?"

"Certainly not," said Nancy quickly. "But it isn't signed and I wondered if the man had claimed to be the artist."

"I think not," Mr. Harlan answered.

"Thank you," Nancy said, and bidding him good-by, she carried the picture to the car. Bess and George exclaimed in delight and examined the portrait while Nancy took the wheel.

"It's a wonderful likeness of Helene," said Bess. "How did the Elite School get the painting?"

Nancy explained and then said, "I want to make sure this is the original. I'll take the painting to Henri and Helene."

"Perhaps they'll be able to identify the red-haired man," George suggested.

The girls stopped for a quick lunch and then went on to Cedar Lake. When they arrived and presented the canvas, the Fontaines were overwhelmed.

"Oh, Nancy, how did you ever find it?" Helene exclaimed. "You are so wonderful!"

"Indeed you are," Henri echoed. "Please tell us everything quickly."

"First, Henri, tell me whether this is the portrait you painted," Nancy requested, "or a copy of it?"

After an examination in a strong light, the artist declared it was his original work.

"But someone has tampered with the picture!"

he declared. "The original paint in several spots has been removed, and replaced with new pigment."

The girls, amazed, looked at the areas of thickly applied impasto that the artist pointed out.

Instantly Nancy remembered the palette knife Judson had dropped at her house. Was he the one who had tampered with the painting? And if so, why?

CHAPTER XII

A Rewarding Hunt

HENRI Fontaine was excited and concerned about the portrait of his sister that had been tampered with.

"It spoils the whole outline of the ruffle, and look what it does to the toe of the slipper," he said. "A botch!"

"Only an expert would know that," George stated. "I think it's a lovely painting."

"It's beautiful," Bess said. "And it looks so real, Helene. Just like you."

But the cousins' remarks failed to mollify the Fontaines. "Someone ruined this painting," said Henri angrily. "But why? Why?"

"Perhaps the paint was used to cover something that was smuggled into the country," Nancy said. "A message, an important chemical formula, or even jewels."

Bess looked skeptical. "How could jewels be hidden in paint?"

Before Nancy could answer, Henri cried excitedly, "Of course they could! I'll show you."

His eyes roved over the outfit each of the three girls was wearing. Finally his glance settled on a novelty pin Bess wore on her blouse.

"May I use this for an experiment?" he asked. "I'll be glad to pay for it."

"That's not necessary," said Bess, handing him the pin. "It's just a piece of inexpensive costume jewelry."

Immediately the young artist started prying loose the settings and took out several of the stones. They were of various sizes, the largest equal to a two-carat diamond.

Henri got a tube of green pigment and squeezed some of it onto a palette. Then he slowly rolled one of the stones around in the paint. When it was completely covered, the artist secreted the mass among the leaves of one of the trees on the canvas. It melted into the background as if it had always been there!

"Why, that's wonderful," Bess said.

Next Henri imbedded several stones into the dancer's frilly tutu. Finally the young man concealed a stone in the toe of one of the scarlet slippers.

"Remarkable," said Helene. "No one would

detect this strange addition to my portrait. Nancy, what does this mean?"

"It's my hunch that a smuggler brought jewels into the United States this way. It is more clever than hiding them in the frame because that would show up in an x-ray, while this method wouldn't. It looks as though Henri's paintings were ordered for the purpose of smuggling. You use the impasto technique, Henri, and that's just what was needed for hiding the jewels."

Henri examined every speck of the old pigment for anything that might still be in it but found nothing.

"Have you any idea about the identity of the smuggler?" Helene asked Nancy.

"Yes," the girl detective answered. "It would explain why Mr. Judson, who isn't an artist, carries a palette knife. As I told my father, I strongly suspect he's really Raoul Amien. What I don't know is how Amien got the painting from Renee and whether Renee is involved in the smuggling."

"If the police want Renee," said George, "he probably is involved. Well, where does the trail take us now?"

To everyone's complete astonishment, Nancy laughed and said, "Into the lake. I'm so warm I can't resist a swim. Does anybody want to join me?"

"In these clothes?" Bess exclaimed.

Nancy announced that during the summer she always carried a bathing suit in the trunk of the convertible and right now she had two with her. Helene had an extra one, so the whole group spent an enjoyable half hour swimming in Cedar Lake.

Later, when Nancy was driving home with Bess and George, she remarked, "Maybe all twelve paintings were used by smugglers. Since the one with the scarlet slippers was sold to a dancing school in this part of the country, some of the others may have been, too. Let's check!"

The girls decided to meet at the Drew home in the morning and take turns telephoning ballet-dancing schools in the state. By the time the cousins arrived, Nancy had a list of fifty. They divided the work and began telephoning.

About halfway through the names George, who was at the telephone, smiled broadly and bobbed her head at the other girls. Into the mouthpiece she said, "Thank you very much. We'll be over to look at it." She replaced the telephone, then said to Nancy and Bess, "One of the pictures is in Harwich. It was sold to the dance studio by a red-haired man."

"Oh, that's marvelous!" said Nancy.

"But Harwich!" Bess exclaimed. "That's almost two hundred miles from River Heights."

"What's two hundred miles?" Nancy asked.

"We'll pack overnight bags and make a real trip out of it—that is, if we can leave our own school that long."

Bess offered to forego the trip and take Nancy's class that afternoon, but the others insisted that she go with them. Finally she arranged with the dancing instructor at a private school in town to conduct the classes.

Late in the morning the girls started out. They had the top down, took turns at the wheel, and enjoyed the bright-blue sky and delightful countryside along the way.

But Nancy did not completely forget the errand on which they had embarked. "I've been thinking a lot about the stolen ballet slippers that belonged to Helene's mother," she remarked. "They must have some special significance."

"Maybe something was hidden in them, too," Bess suggested.

"Possibly. But it's strange that neither Helene nor Henri knew about it."

The girls reached Harwich late in the afternoon and drove immediately to the attractive building that housed the Harwich School of the Dance. As Nancy and her friends walked into the reception room, they saw Helene's portrait in a prominent position on the wall.

"How lovely!" Bess murmured.

The painting portrayed the girl in a graceful

glissade. It was so realistic, Helene looked as though she were about to glide right off the canvas.

An attractive, blond woman in a ballet costume came forward and introduced herself as Miss Desmond, the director of the school. George identified herself as the one who had talked with her on the telephone that morning and introduced Nancy and Bess. Then she added, "Nancy is an amateur detective. She's investigating a case we think involves the smuggling of precious stones. We believe that they were hidden in the pigment of certain pictures. Yours may be one of them."

"Oh, dear!" Miss Desmond exclaimed. "I hope this won't involve me. I know nothing about the smuggled gems."

"I didn't mean to imply that," said George. She regretted having been so blunt.

"This must be a shock to you," Nancy added understandingly. "But would you mind if we examine the picture closely?"

Her quick eye had detected a spot where the pigment had been tampered with.

"Go ahead," Miss Desmond said.

Nancy took a small magnifying glass from her handbag and scrutinized the painting.

"Something has been removed from the picture, I'm sure," she said after a moment. "And,"

Nancy added, her voice excited, "if I'm not mistaken, there is still one stone hidden!"

"What!" Miss Desmond exclaimed in disbelief.

Nancy pointed to the spot and asked, "Will you let me prove it?"

"Why, certainly, but you don't think I——" the worried director began.

Nancy smiled at the woman. "We believe you bought the picture without knowing all this."

Miss Desmond looked relieved and watched as Nancy took the palette knife with the initial R on it from her bag and began to scrape the white pigment in one ruffle of the skirt. Finally a large lump came off in her hand. She scraped at it even faster. A moment later she uncovered a sparkling diamond!

"I just can't believe it!" Miss Desmond cried, as Bess and George gasped. "I-I certainly got my money's worth, didn't I?" Then instantly an expression of alarm crossed her face. "But I may be holding stolen property! What shall I do with the stone?"

"I'd suggest," said Nancy, "that you come with me to the Harwich Police Station and leave the diamond there until the case is cleared up."

The dancing-school director said the sooner she got rid of the diamond, and the painting too, the better! Miss Desmond was glad to sell the painting to Nancy for ten dollars.

She accompanied Nancy to the police station, while the cousins remained at the school to admit the next class of pupils. The director sighed when the ordeal was over.

"Thank you, Nancy, for getting me out of an embarrassing situation," she said. "And good luck in solving the mystery."

Nancy, Bess, and George spent the night in a hotel in Harwich. They started on their return journey early the next morning, with the painting stored in the trunk. As they drove along—all three girls on the front seat—they discussed the various facets of the case.

Presently Nancy said, "I have a strange feeling that those little figurines that were sold to Mr. Howard, the jeweler, were also used to smuggle jewels into this country—maybe by the same group."

"And Mr. Warte removed them and tried to patch up the cracks?" Bess suggested.

"Yes."

Hours later, as Nancy took a road leading away from River Heights, George pointed out that Nancy had taken the wrong turn.

"I know," said Nancy. "I thought we'd stop to see Helene and Henri and leave this picture."

Presently they turned into the woods road leading to the Nickerson cabin. Nancy had to drive slowly because of the twists and turns on the winding trail.

Rounding a sharp curve, Nancy almost ran into a barrier across the road. A bridge over a stream was down and sawhorses had been set up to warn motorists.

As Nancy jammed on the brake, George said in disgust, "Well, of all things! Why didn't they put up a sign where we entered this road?"

"What'll we do, Nancy?" Bess asked. "Walk the rest of the way?"

"I suppose so," Nancy said.

She had her hand on the door handle to turn it when a voice behind the girls called in a heavy French accent, "Do not turn around! You are my prisoners and will do exactly what I tell you!"

CHAPTER XIII

"Officer, Help!"

THE unseen speaker hopped into the rear seat of Nancy's convertible.

Obeying his instructions, the three girls had not turned around, but in the rearview mirror Nancy had caught sight of the cruel-looking man. He was the person she had come to know as Judson!

"Clever of me, wasn't it, to pick up your trail?" he boasted. "I've been following you for miles, hoping for a chance to stop you. I thought you might turn in here, because you've done so before. I knew the bridge was out and hurried ahead of you to take down the warning sign at the entrance to the road." He laughed sardonically.

The next moment Bess screamed. Judson had shoved a sharp palette knife between her face and Nancy's! He withdrew it, then said, "One false move and I'll use this to advantage! You'd better believe me so don't test your luck."

Bess looked faint and George's jaw was set grimly. Nancy, after the first shock was over, said evenly, "What do you want us to do?"

"You are going to be nice young ladies and lead me to the Fontaines!"

Nancy thought quickly. Her first idea was to get the man out of the convertible.

"What about your car?" she asked, wondering where it was. She could not see it in the mirror.

Judson laughed harshly. "I know how clever you are, Nancy Drew. I am not falling for your trick to get me out of this car so that you and your friends can escape. Now back up and don't get any crazy ideas."

Nancy nudged Bess and murmured, "Don't worry!" She put the car into reverse and backed out of the winding road. Judson's car was hidden just beyond the bend.

In spite of their predicament, the young sleuth felt a sense of satisfaction. Judson's desperate action clearly indicated that he did not know where the Fontaines were hiding!

Nancy sensed, too, that one of the reasons he wanted to ride in the car was that he did not care to walk through the woods with the three girls. In a struggle to get free, his prisoners would be more than a match for him!

At the main road, Nancy decided to stay on the

highway as long as Judson would allow it, hoping to meet a State Police patrol car. But she had driven only a short distance when Judson said, "I know the Fontaines aren't hidden along the highway. Get off it and lead me to them! Be quick about it!"

George had surmised Nancy's plan. Carefully concealing her action, she slipped a note pad and pencil out of her purse. Holding it on her lap where Judson could not see it, George wrote, "Do you want Bess and me to tackle him?"

Nancy glanced at the note. Slowly taking her right hand from the wheel, she wrote, "Not yet."

As she continued to drive with one hand, Judson evidently noticed her right hand was out of sight. He placed the point of the palette knife between Nancy's shoulders and barked, "Keep both hands on the wheel, where I can see them!"

Nancy complied immediately and turned into a side road. The knife was removed. The young detective knew the countryside around River Heights well. She recalled that Bert Fraser, a state trooper, lived on one of the back lanes in the vicinity.

"I'll head for his house and hope he'll be there," she said to herself.

Nancy took the road leading to the Fraser home. As they went farther and farther from the highway, Judson apparently was pleased.

"Keep both hands on the wheel, where I can see them!"

Nancy smiled when she saw one corner of the trooper's house appear at the top of a hill.

When they neared it and Nancy began to slow down, Judson said, "Are the Fontaines here?"

Nancy did not answer. She braked the car to a stop near the front porch. At almost the same moment, the trooper opened the door and came out, dressed in full uniform. Nancy and George already had the car doors open on each side and jumped out.

Bess cried, "Officer, we're being kidnapped!"

"Kidnapped?" the trooper exclaimed, running down the steps.

At the same instant Judson made a flying leap over the back of the car, and sprinted toward the woods on the opposite side of the road.

"We must catch him!" Nancy urged.

The officer and the three girls dashed among the trees in pursuit of Judson. They could hear him crashing through the underbrush. As they ran on, Nancy gasped out her story.

At a clearing near the brow of the hill they caught a glimpse of the man. Officer Fraser shouted at him to stop, but Judson ignored the command. He swerved to one side and again plunged into the cover of the woods.

They zigzagged through the woods for fifteen minutes. Suddenly Nancy realized that they were chasing the man directly toward the Nickerson cabin! She warned the others, saying, "It would be better to let him go than have him find the Fontaines! Let's give up the chase. Then maybe he'll head for the main road. His car is hidden back where he stopped us."

"All right," the policeman agreed. "I have my radio car at the house. I'll go back and send out a general alarm. You can follow at your leisure."

Nancy and George felt as fresh as ever, but poor Bess was panting and insisted upon resting a few minutes. By the time they reached Bert Fraser's home, he had already contacted headquarters.

"I think we have him bottled up," the officer told them. "The police will set a trap for him."

"Thanks for helping us," Nancy said. "I'm sorry I let Judson slip through my fingers."

The trooper smiled. "Would you like to go along with me and help us capture him?"

Nancy beamed. "I sure would! At least I'd like to talk to Judson." She turned to Bess and George. "Shall we follow in my car or would you two rather take the convertible and go home? I could ride with Mr. Fraser."

"We'll see this thing through," George declared.

"Stay close behind me," Fraser directed, "And, Miss Drew, suppose you ride in my car."

Nancy climbed in with the trooper and they drove off. She was fascinated by the constant exchange of information over the radio between

State Police headquarters and the individual patrol cars.

When they reached the main highway, she looked back to make certain that the cousins were following. The girls waved to indicate that everything was fine.

The trip to the Cedar Lake road was rapid. Another police car was already there. Bert Fraser jumped out and ran over to talk to his colleagues. In a few minutes he was back.

"Judson's car was gone when they arrived," he told Nancy. "He must have made a fast getaway!"

Nancy was not sure that it was Judson who had taken the car. He might have had an accomplice. She decided to find out whether or not Judson had found the Fontaines.

"I think the girls and I will call on friends of ours who are staying at a cabin on the lake," she told the trooper. "Thank you for all your help."

Nancy explained her plan to Bess and George, who had pulled up in back of the officer's car. They got out, crossed the stream on its temporary footbridge, and walked to the Nickerson cabin.

As they approached the cabin, Nancy's heart sank. No one was sitting on the porch. And although it was a warm day, every window in the cabin was closed. The boats were tied up at the wharf, and the lakefront was deserted. There was an eerie stillness about the area.

Nancy hastened to try the front door of the

cabin. It was locked. A check showed that all the windows and the rear door were locked as well. Instantly worried looks appeared on the three girls' faces.

"Judson got here first!" Bess wailed. "He's kidnapped Helene and Henri!"

CHAPTER XIV

Puzzling Phone Calls

WHILE Nancy was trying to form her own opinion about the Fontaines' absence from the cabin, George said hesitantly, "Perhaps we were wrong to trust Helene and Henri. They may be part of the smuggling gang. When Henri realized that you had discovered that impasto technique for hiding gems, he may have decided to disappear. You'll have to admit he was skillful in hiding the stones from Bess's pin."

Bess defended the Fontaines. "If that's so, why would someone in the gang send them warning notes and steal Helene's scarlet slippers?"

Nancy agreed with Bess. "I still think the Fontaines have fled *from* Judson, not *with* him."

The girls walked along the porch and peered through the windows. Nancy's half-finished portrait lay upside down on the floor. Furniture had been overturned and a footstool was leaning against an andiron in the open fireplace.

"I think we should investigate further!" Nancy declared. She opened the cabin door with a spare key the Nickersons always left in the hollow of a tree.

The girls found that the Fontaines' luggage was still in their rooms.

"Perhaps Henri and Helene just went out for a hike in the woods," George suggested. "And Judson may have been in here and upset the furniture while hunting for something."

On the chance that she was right, the girls waited for several hours. The Fontaines did not appear. When the girls left, Nancy propped a note against a lamp: *Scarlet, let me hear from you.*

No message came that evening. By morning, Nancy was forced to admit that the Fontaines had vanished. Was it voluntarily, or by force?

The young detective was bewildered. All clues seemed to have come to naught, and she had no idea where to begin looking for the Fontaines. Then she remembered her newspaper advertisement.

"Hannah," she said after breakfast, "I'm going down to the *Gazette* office."

Nancy found that she had received four letters. The first three she opened described pictures of ballet dancers, but none sounded like the ones Henri had painted of his sister.

The fourth letter was unsigned and mysterious. Nancy read it several times without understanding it. Finally she drove to her father's office.

Mr. Drew was also puzzled as he read, " 'If you will put a personal advertisement in the *Gazette,* including the word artist and your telephone number in reverse, the writer of this note will have an interesting story to relate about a painting of a lovely ballet dancer posing before a forest background.' "

"That sounds like one of the pictures of Helene," Nancy said. "What do you think of the note, Dad?"

Mr. Drew leaned back in his chair, drummed his fingers on the desk, and remarked, "It's possible someone from Centrovia read your ad. To avoid undercover agents of the occupation authorities, this person may not want to reveal his identity or whereabouts until he's sure he's not dealing with one of them. I can see no harm in your answering the note."

Mr. Drew went on to say that he would get in touch with a friend in the telephone company and have an additional line run into the house that afternoon. He would be able to use it to trace the strange call.

Nancy wrote out the advertisement in accordance with the instructions in the note, and took it to the *Gazette* office. She then returned home and told Hannah Gruen about the mysterious note and the telephone call, which would probably come the next morning. "You can help," she added.

"How?" asked the housekeeper.

Nancy explained that while she was talking on the hall phone, her father would try to trace the call on the private phone he was having installed in his study.

"I'd like you to run back and forth between Dad and me with messages," Nancy requested.

A few minutes after nine the next morning, the phone rang. Hannah followed Mr. Drew into his study. Nancy picked up the phone in the hall and heard a voice with a foreign accent.

"Is this the person who placed a personal ad in the *Gazette?*"

"That's right," Nancy answered.

"Are you an American?" was the next question.

"Yes," Nancy replied. "I was born here in River Heights. Why do you ask?"

The speaker ignored her question and went on, "Are you connected with the police?"

Nancy thought this was a strange question, but answered truthfully, "I have many friends on the police force, but have no official connection with them. However, I do like to solve mysteries."

Nancy could not rid herself of the opinion that the voice sounded like Johann Koff's. Could the speaker be the person who had sent her father to New York on a wild-goose chase?

Hannah came out of the study and whispered, "He is calling from a phone booth in a Cliffwood drugstore."

Nancy covered the mouthpiece and said, "Tell Dad it sounds like Mr. Koff."

At that moment Hannah glanced out the window. She said in a low voice, "It can't be Mr. Koff. He just went by in a car."

Nancy nodded, then continued her conversation with the unknown speaker. "What is the interesting story about your painting?"

"It will probably seem sentimental and romantic coming from a man," the speaker said, a trace of a chuckle in his voice. "I purchased the picture because the girl in it reminded me of a dancer in my native country."

"What country is that?" Nancy asked, as if she were just being polite.

"A little country that is probably unknown to you," the man replied. "Centrovia."

Nancy paused, hoping her voice would not betray her excitement. "I have heard of Centrovia. Did the painting come from there?"

"No, I bought it in this country. But since I have had the picture in my possession, I have learned something rather disturbing about it."

"Yes?" said Nancy eagerly.

"I do not wish to discuss it on the telephone. But I would like very much to talk to you."

Nancy was relieved to hear her father coming to her side. She covered the telephone as he said, "I've made a check on him with the owner of the drugstore where he put in the call. He seems to be all right."

Nancy turned back to the phone. "You've certainly aroused my curiosity, Mr.—— er—— I didn't get your name."

"Anton Schmidt. I am an amateur artist. May I see you and talk to you about this soon?"

Nancy gave the caller her name and address, and asked, "Can you come to my home this evening?"

They agreed on eight o'clock, and Anton Schmidt arrived promptly at that hour. He was pleasant-looking and resembled Mr. Koff, though he was several years younger. He carried the bulky painting, carefully wrapped in brown paper.

After they had exchanged a few pleasantries in the Drew living room, Nancy asked, "Are you by any chance related to another Centrovian by the name of Johann Koff?"

Schmidt's eyes widened. "Indeed I am. He is my cousin. But how do you happen to know him? I've been out of touch with him for more than ten years. Before the occupation he lived in a neighboring province in our country, and was still there the last I heard."

Nancy told Mr. Schmidt that his cousin was now living in River Heights. "If you would like to see him, I'll phone him and ask him to come right over. He's living at the Claymore Hotel."

"That would be a great pleasure."

Nancy made the call. Mr. Koff was surprised at the news and promised to hurry over at once.

"Anton! Little Anton! I can hardly believe it. I will see you in a few minutes."

When Nancy returned to the living room, Mr. Schmidt had unwrapped the painting. It was another portrait of Helene Fontaine.

"I bought this in a little gift shop out in the country," he explained. "The girl who modeled for it looks very much like Madame Provak, a famous ballet dancer whom I saw perform many years ago, before the trouble in our country. I have not seen or heard of her since."

After a pause, the caller smiled and said to Nancy, "Do you mind if I ask why you are searching for paintings of a ballerina?"

"I am an amateur detective, and my father is a lawyer," Nancy replied. "We are working together on a case that involves the children of Madame Provak."

"You know them? Where are they?"

Nancy told of her connection with Henri and

Helene Fontaine. "The girl in this painting," she went on, "is Helene, the daughter of the famous dancer you knew. Her parents passed away some years ago in France. Later, Helene and her brother were threatened and fled to this country."

Mr. Schmidt's brow furrowed. "This painting is unsigned," he said. "I am anxious to learn the artist's name."

Mr. Drew nodded to signal to his daughter that he thought it would be safe to reveal the truth.

"Henri painted it," Nancy declared.

The caller gasped. "Miss Drew, I must now tell you the strange story I mentioned over the telephone. As you know, I am an amateur artist. In examining this portrait closely, I discovered that two valuable gems had been hidden in the pigment that forms the ruffles of the ballet skirt. I was about to go to the police with my find when I happened to see your ad."

Nancy and her father exchanged glances. Each was thinking how careless the smugglers were, not to have removed all the gems!

"Your find," said Mr. Drew, "confirms a suspicion of ours that jewels were smuggled into this country from France by this method."

Mr. Schmidt jumped excitedly from his chair. "This may explain a great theft of gems from the leaders of the Centrovian underground movement."

Nancy and her father instantly thought of the jewels carried to France by the Provaks. Had some of these been stolen?

Mr. Schmidt went on to say that the Provaks had had spotless reputations, so far as he knew. However, life might have become so hard for the brother and sister that they had resorted to thievery of the last of the jewels their parents had turned over to the Centrovian underground, and smuggled them into the United States.

"Oh, I'm sure Helene and Henri are honest," Nancy cried. "Mr. Schmidt, have you any idea who sold the painting to the gift shop where you purchased it?"

The girl was elated when she heard that Mr. Schmidt had learned from the proprietor that the man had red hair.

The conversation was interrupted suddenly by the arrival of Mr. Koff, who rushed across the room and clasped Anton Schmidt in his arms.

"Anton!"

"Johann!"

Finally Mr. Koff turned to the others and said, "You must think we are very emotional, but this is a most happy occasion."

The Drews smiled understandingly. Then they told the story of Schmidt's painting.

"This does look bad for Helene and Henri," Mr. Koff agreed. "It was for such things as this that I was so worried about losing my briefcase."

He explained the loss to his cousin and added, "I am afraid that letters in it that mentioned the stolen jewels have fallen into the thieves' hands. They may be trying to shift the blame for the theft and the smuggling onto the Fontaines, and for the third time have frightened them away."

The new complications in the case worried everyone. But both Centrovians expressed a hearty certainty that the Fontaines would prove to be honest.

"As evidence of my good faith," said Mr. Schmidt, "I would like to leave this portrait and the gems here for safekeeping."

Although the Drews knew this might involve them more deeply in the situation, they agreed to be custodians of the articles.

The next morning, Nancy received a startling telegram, a night letter from Cliffwood. "Why, listen to this, Hannah!" she exclaimed, and read:

YOUR HELP NO LONGER NEEDED. ANY CONTINUED INTEREST IN OUR CASE ON YOUR PART WILL PROVE EMBARRASSING TO US AND DANGEROUS TO YOU.

HELENE.

"Well, that's gratitude for you!" Hannah remarked. "Never a thank you!"

Before Nancy had a chance to respond, the telephone rang. The girl answered it.

A weak, frightened voice asked, "N-Nancy?"

"Yes. Who——?"

"This is Helene. Please come right away to——"

There was a scream and the sound of a crash as though the instrument had been torn from Helene's grasp. Then the line went dead!

CHAPTER XV

A Chase

NANCY sat still for several minutes, pondering the telegram and the phone call. The messages were completely contradictory. One of them was a fake. But which one?

"Hannah," said Nancy, after returning to the breakfast table and telling her about the call, "I'm going to drive over to Cliffwood and see if I can learn anything about the sender of that telegram."

"All right, dear, but do be careful."

On the way Nancy spotted George strolling on the main street and asked her to go along. When Nancy told her about the latest developments in the case, George whistled.

"Sounds as if Helene and Henri really have been kidnapped."

Nancy nodded.

At the Cliffwood telegraph office she explained

to the clerk that she suspected a hoax. The woman was very cooperative and checked the original message. The sender had refused to give an address.

"It was a counter telegram," she explained, "written here and paid for in cash. I have no way of tracing the sender. I do recall that it was filed by a woman, though—kind of loud in her dress and speech. Does that help you?"

"Very much," said Nancy, her mind instantly conjuring up a picture of Mrs. Judson.

Nancy went back to the car and relayed the information to George.

"I'll bet," said George emphatically, "that this whole business was staged."

"In what way?"

"Both the telegram and the phone call," George replied, "were sent to sidetrack you from the case." George chuckled. "But they don't know Nancy Drew and the way she thrives on challenges. But where has this one led us? Into a blind alley."

Nancy smiled, then said, "When I run into a dead end on a clue, I go back to the beginning and start all over again."

"The beginning?" George repeated. "You mean all the way back to the bisque figurines?"

"That's as good a place as any, George."

The girls had lunch; then Nancy drove back to

River Heights. George left her, and Nancy went to her father's office. After describing the morning's happenings, she made a request.

"Dad, would you please find out from customs if those bisque figurines were imported? I suspect they as well as the paintings may have been shipped to Mr. Duparc."

"I can try," the lawyer readily agreed.

Nancy said she would be at the dancing school if he should want her, and headed for the Fontaines' studio. She found things running smoothly, with Mrs. Nickerson in charge. Since there were twenty minutes before the next class, Nancy donned a leotard and practiced for her dance in the forthcoming charity show.

"That's excellent," Ned's mother commented enthusiastically after watching her.

When Nancy's class of young students arrived and had gotten into their costumes, she began a story she loved about the great ballerina Pavlova.

"One of Pavlova's favorite dances," Nancy said, "was called 'The Swan.' It's said she floated across the stage in a filmy white-feathered costume even more gracefully than this lovely bird swims! And how do you think Pavlova learned to imitate it?"

"How?" chorused the little girls.

"In her garden at Ivy House in Hampstead, England," Nancy said, "Pavlova had a small lake with tame swans swimming on it. She used to watch them for hours, and sometimes she caressed her beautiful white birds and let them fly back to the water. She watched every movement."

"Did she have any other pets?" Susie asked.

"Yes," said Nancy. "Pavlova had a gorgeous cockatoo that she loved to feed grapes. By the way, how many of you girls have watched the swans in our own River Heights park?"

All of them raised their hands and Nancy said, "How about all of you pretending to be swans and using the steps you've been learning?"

The children were eager to try it, so Nancy put on a recording of *Swan Lake* and the little girls began to flit around the room, gliding, swimming, diving.

When the class was over, Mrs. Nickerson called Nancy to the phone. "It's Ned," she told her and handed over the instrument.

"Hello, Ned."

"Hi, Nancy! How about a late afternoon ride and dinner with me? You need a rest from the Fontaine case."

Nancy agreed to go. She put on her pink sports dress and helped Mrs. Nickerson with some of the clerical work until Ned arrived. As they pulled away from the curb, she said, "Please, Ned, if it doesn't make any great difference where we go, let's drive to Cliffwood."

"Why Cliffwood?"

"Mrs. Judson sent me a telegram from there.

Maybe that's where she and her husband are living."

Ned groaned in mock annoyance but admitted he would enjoy helping Nancy solve at least part of the mystery. Arriving in Cliffwood, he began a patrol of the streets. They had just passed the railroad station and were nearing a big supermarket when Nancy suddenly gripped Ned's arm.

"There's Mrs. Judson now, going into that store across the street!"

Ned stopped the car and Nancy jumped out. Traffic was heavy and delayed her. Finally she crossed to the far side and hurried into the market, which was crowded with shoppers.

Nancy looked quickly down one aisle and then the next. By the time she located Mrs. Judson, who was wearing a bright-green dress, the mysterious woman had completed her purchases and was at the check-out counter, paying her bill.

The width of the store and half-loaded carts in awkward positions were between her and Nancy. Nancy made her way among them as fast as she could, but when she reached the exit, Mrs. Judson was already leaving the store.

At the check-out counter, Nancy tried to push her way through the line of carts and customers. An irate cashier looked up and said, "Wait your turn, miss! These customers are in a hurry, too."

"I'm not buying anything," Nancy told her, and as several women glowered at her, she finally broke into the clear and headed for the doorway.

By the time she reached the street, Mrs. Judson was at the railroad station. Nancy heard a train coming and looked around wildly for Ned. He was not in sight.

Nancy raced across the street to the station. As she dashed through the waiting room, she caught sight of Mrs. Judson on the train, which was just pulling out. Nancy had no chance to climb aboard.

"But I mustn't lose that woman!" she said to herself.

As Nancy headed for the taxi stand with the thought of catching the train at the next station, Ned pulled up and called, "Going my way, lady?"

Nancy jumped into the car quickly and explained what had happened. Ned took up the chase.

"I'd like to make a suggestion," he said. "Don't board that train. That woman will be sure to make a scene. We'll follow her until she gets off and then tackle her."

"All right, Ned."

They met the train at the next three stations, and each time checked the descending passengers. Mrs. Judson was not among them.

"Next stop, Brandon!" said Ned cheerfully, continuing the chase.

The train was slowing to a stop at Brandon when Nancy left the car and hurried toward the tracks. A moment later Mrs. Judson alighted and headed for the street.

Nancy dashed to her side and grabbed the woman's arm. "Good afternoon, Mrs. Judson," she said. "I've been looking for you."

Mrs. Judson whirled and tried to break Nancy's grasp. But the young detective held on tightly. In the scuffle that followed, Mrs. Judson's handbag opened.

Out tumbled the scarlet ballet slippers!

The stiff toes had been pulled apart. Quickly Nancy concluded that Mrs. Judson must have stolen the slippers because something was secreted in them. She wondered if the woman had found it.

At this point Ned hurried up with a policeman. "Arrest this woman!" the young man ordered.

"What's the charge?" the officer asked.

"The theft of these ballet shoes," Nancy replied. "This woman uses the name of Mrs. Judson, but I don't think that's her right name. Federal authorities are looking for her and her husband in connection with a smuggling racket. These slippers have something to do with it."

The policeman was open-mouthed with astonishment. But before he could act, Mrs. Judson screamed, "My husband is no smuggler! This girl is lying to cover herself."

"What do you mean, ma'am?"

Mrs. Judson cried defiantly, "This Nancy Drew calls herself a detective. But she's a law-breaker!"

"What makes you say that?" the policeman demanded.

"She accuses my husband and me of being smugglers when actually she is shielding the real smugglers. Make her tell you where they are!"

CHAPTER XVI

Disguise

It occurred to Nancy that if she could keep Mrs. Judson talking, the woman might reveal something vital.

"Officer," she said, "I suggest we go to police headquarters and talk to the chief."

"All right, miss." He took Mrs. Judson by the arm and escorted her to Captain Crane's office. Nancy and Ned followed.

Nancy told the bald-headed, round-faced chief of the theft of the scarlet slippers, and of her certainty that Mrs. Judson and her husband were involved in a smuggling racket.

As the young detective finished, the woman cried out in a loud, twangy voice, "Chief, this girl's crazy! My husband and I never stole anything in our lives, and as for smuggling jewels into this country——"

Mrs. Judson stopped speaking, covered with

confusion. Not once had Nancy mentioned jewels! The suspect had given herself away!

Nancy said that the woman's husband used the name David Judson, also Raoul Amien.

Mrs. Judson sprang across the room toward Nancy. "The police will never find him! I'll never tell where he is!" she screamed.

She tried to claw Nancy, but Ned restrained her. When the fracas was over, he said, "Captain, I think you may know Nancy Drew by reputation. Her father is Carson Drew, a lawyer in River Heights."

"Indeed I do," the officer replied. "I've read about your exploits as a detective, Miss Drew." He smiled. "If our department can help you in this smuggling case, we'll certainly do all we can. But first, if you'll file a formal complaint of theft, I'll have Mrs. Judson held."

After the woman had been put in a cell, Captain Crane said, "I'll keep the scarlet slippers as evidence, and I'll personally see that any callers Mrs. Judson has are examined carefully. And now, is there any other way I can help you?"

"Perhaps," Nancy said. "I suspect that in connection with the case there has been a kidnapping of a brother and sister who run a dancing school in River Heights. Can you think of any place in Brandon where they might be held prisoners without arousing too much attention?"

Captain Crane said he knew of none, but would ask some of his patrolmen.

He took his callers into the squad room and put the same question to the half-dozen shirt-sleeved men there. All shook their heads except one, who said, "There's an old two-story farmhouse on the edge of Brandon that was abandoned until recently. I don't know who's taken it."

"We might find out, Donovan," Captain Crane decided. "You ride out there with these young folks and see if there's anything suspicious about the place."

They drove out in Ned's car. The house stood a distance from the road on a lane bordered by woods. As the callers stopped, they were met by a stooped limping old man with white hair, a mustache and bright, dark eyes. He wore light-blue trousers and a faded checkered sports jacket.

Officer Donovan spoke to him, but apparently the man was stone deaf, for he shakily handed the officer a pencill and pad.

Donovan wrote, "Who lives here?"

The man read the question, then penciled, "My wife and me. Name is Brown. She is away."

Nancy made no comment as they headed back to police headquarters. But when she and Ned were alone, the young sleuth said, "Let's go back to the farmhouse. That old man isn't deaf."

"How do you know?" asked Ned, amazed.

Nancy smiled. "Before we reached him, I saw the man turn his head when a dog barked in the distance."

"And I'll bet you think the old-man stuff is faked, too," Ned said with a chuckle.

"Yes, I do. And he's not dumb."

This time, Ned stopped the car a quarter of a mile from the farmhouse and the couple approached cautiously on foot. From the woods, Nancy studied the upper floor of the house for some sign that prisoners might be concealed behind the curtained windows. But she saw nothing suspicious. Their knock was not answered.

"Maybe the man is out but will come back," Nancy suggested. "Let's wait over there in the shade."

Fifteen minutes went by before their patience was rewarded. Then the man, still wearing the light-blue trousers and faded sports jacket, stepped out the front door into the yard.

But he was no longer an old man! The white hair was now shiny black and the mustache was gone. As the man stood, tall and erect, he looked thinner and more gaunt than he had in his disguise as a farmer. There was no mistaking his eyes, though.

The man was a complete stranger to Nancy. To prove her point about his hearing, the girl whistled and the man turned around. Nancy and Ned stepped forward.

"What was the idea of the disguise?" Ned demanded.

The man was shocked for a moment, then relaxed and smiled disarmingly. In a French accent he replied, "You are detectives?"

"Amateurs," Nancy answered.

"Very good. I am one myself. If you will come in and sit down, I will tell my story. Perhaps we can work together."

Ned spoke quickly. "The porch steps will do."

Nancy could see he did not trust the stranger. She would have liked to look at the inside of the house for clues that might connect the Frenchman with the Fontaines or with the smuggling racket. But she said nothing.

"I am here from France on an important mission," the man began. "I am not well acquainted with the methods of American police and so have not consulted them. It seemed to me that a disguise would be the best way to find a couple I am looking for."

"Yes?" Nancy urged as he stopped speaking.

"This couple," the French detective went on, "is responsible for smuggling many gems from my native France. I have traced them."

"To Brandon?" Nancy prompted.

"Not exactly." The Frenchman hesitated for a

moment. "To River Heights. You know River Heights?"

Nancy felt the need of caution in revealing anything, but Ned said, "Yes. And would your suspects, by any chance, call themselves the David Judsons?"

"But no," the Frenchman replied. "The smugglers I am looking for are named Henri and Helene Fontaine!"

CHAPTER XVII

Ned's Ruse

In spite of herself, Nancy gasped at the Frenchman's announcement.

"You know the Fontaines?" he asked hopefully.

Nancy countered with, "Are they the ones who used to be in River Heights?"

"Yes. Where are they now?"

"I don't know. But please tell me more about the smuggling. It's unbelievable," Nancy said.

The man gave her a long, searching stare, then replied, "This Henri Fontaine is an artist. Quite a clever one. In Paris, he was contacted by an art dealer named Tomas Renee, who ordered twelve pictures from Monsieur Fontaine."

"What sort of pictures?" Nancy asked.

"They were portraits of a ballet dancer in twelve different poses," the Frenchman replied. "The Fontaine girl is a very capable ballet dancer and posed for the pictures."

"That sounds like a convenient arrangement," Ned remarked noncommittally. "Where did Renee sell the portraits?"

"They were to be entered in a race among art dealers for an order from a famous dancing school. But before this could take place, every one of the pictures was stolen!"

"And Renee had no idea who had stolen them?" Ned asked.

The Frenchman threw up his arms in a helpless gesture, then replied, "Not at the time. But he does now."

"Please go on," Nancy requested as the man paused.

"When the police failed, Renee asked every art dealer in France to help him. The pictures were so unusual in content and treatment that they would be readily recognizable. But no one in France had any inkling of where they were."

"And then?" said Nancy.

"Renee talked it over with some of his friends," the Frenchman declared. "He decided that if the portraits were not in France, then they must have been shipped abroad. I checked with customs and made a startling discovery."

Nancy looked up quickly. "Yes?"

"I learned," the Frenchman explained, "that a young man fitting the description of Henri Fontaine had used the name of Renee to send eleven of the pictures to the United States."

"How amazing!" Ned exclaimed.

"Why eleven pictures?" Nancy asked. "What became of the twelfth?"

The Frenchman shrugged. "Who knows?" he said. "Perhaps it was stolen from Henri Fontaine. Or he may have sold it in order to secure funds for some of his undercover activities."

"Undercover?" Nancy repeated, but the man did not explain.

Nancy leaned back against the step, looked up at the sky, and closed her eyes. She was recalling descriptions of various people in the case. Suddenly she remembered the Fontaines' description of Renee as a tall, thin, gaunt-looking fellow.

Nancy straightened up. Could this man be Renee? She must find out! Smiling, she said, "As an amateur detective I could almost believe that you are Tomas Renee."

The man started. Then he said, "You are a clever and observant young lady. Yes, I am Tomas Renee."

It was Nancy's turn to be amazed. She had fully expected the man to deny it.

"You seem surprised," he said, amused. "I have nothing to hide. But I wanted to make sure you were to be trusted before I revealed my identity. Now let us get down to work."

"What about the jewel smuggling?" Nancy reminded him.

"Oh, yes. I am inclined to think that the jewels

were connected with the portraits. At the same time that the twelve paintings disappeared from my gallery, a large quantity of valuable gems was stolen in a suburb of Paris. They may have been secreted in the frames before the portraits were sent to this country."

"Then you merely suspect the Fontaines," Nancy remarked. "You do not have any clear evidence pointing to them as the jewel smugglers."

"Perhaps you are right," the Frenchman conceded. "But the Fontaines also disappeared at that very time!"

"I see," said Nancy, rising. "Well, if I can help you, I'll let you know."

Renee and Ned also rose and the Frenchman said, "I have the hunch, as you call it, that you young people will solve this mystery for me. And whom have I the honor of working with? What are your names?"

Before Nancy could say anything, Ned gripped her arm and then asked Renee, "Did you ever hear of the Colemans?"

Tomas Renee shook his head slowly. Nancy was puzzled by Ned's ruse, especially since she recalled that Coleman was his middle name.

Ned went on, "I think we'd better be on our way, dear. We can contact Mr. Renee later on if we learn anything about the Fontaines or his missing portraits."

Half dragging and half pushing her, Ned started off through the woods. They had not gone far when Nancy asked for an explanation of what he had done.

"I don't trust that guy," Ned replied.

"But what was the idea of giving him an impression like that?"

"Impression like what?" Ned asked in some surprise.

"Anyone who heard you would think we're husband and wife. Especially a man like Renee."

Ned laughed heartily. "Well, someday I hope it'll be true. And for your information I hope he'll think we're married now. If he's a spy or a kidnapper, as I suspect, he'd better not find out your name is Drew!"

Nancy agreed and said she did not trust Renee either.

Ned remarked, "He didn't have to tell us that long story. I'll bet he wouldn't have admitted his identity if you hadn't asked him. The less he knows about us, the better!"

Nancy smiled then, took Ned's arm in her own, and said, "You're on the warpath, aren't you?"

"Yes, and I'm going to do something about it," he declared. "I want you to walk to the car and drive to police headquarters. Get hold of Captain Crane and a couple of his patrolmen and bring them back here. I'm sure Renee's story won't stand up when the police question him about his activities. I'll return to the house and keep him there."

"If Renee plays innocent," said Nancy, starting off, "at least we can have the house searched. Helene and Henri may be there. Somehow, Ned, I just can't bring myself to believe they're guilty of this jewel smuggling."

"Nor can I," said Ned.

He left her, and Nancy hurried on toward the car. She had nearly reached the road when suddenly a coat was thrown forcefully over her head and both hands were pinned behind her.

Nancy screamed but the sound was too muffled to carry far.

"So you are Nancy Drew!" her captor snarled. "Double-crosser! You will never notify the police, and you will be sorry you ever tried it!"

CHAPTER XVIII

A Dancer's Footprints

RENEE snatched the keys to Ned's car from Nancy's hand and whipped a rope from his pocket. Nancy fought unsuccessfully to free herself.

Renee mumbled to himself while he was binding Nancy. She caught a word here and there. ". . . their car must be at the end of this trail she and her boyfriend made—I'll move it. Nobody will find it until after I escape."

When the young sleuth's hands and ankles were securely bound, the man dragged her through the woods. Stones and twigs scratched her, and she gritted her teeth against the pain. In a few minutes Renee stopped and Nancy heard a car door open. She was lifted off the ground and shoved onto the floor behind the front seat.

Renee drove the car down a rough, twisting

road. Nancy guessed that he was running it deep into the woods to hide it.

Presently the man stopped the car with a jerk and turned off the ignition. He snatched the coat from Nancy's head, and before she could scream for help, stuffed a gag in her mouth.

Glaring at the girl, Renee said, "You will mind your own business from now on and not interfere with mine! If you disobey, I shall not be so easy on you the next time."

He rolled up all the windows and slammed the door shut, leaving Nancy huddled on the floor. At first she struggled, but as the car became stuffy, she began to feel faint.

"Oh, I hope Ned is more watchful than I was," she said to herself. "Renee must have followed us and heard us talking."

One thought after another whirled through the young sleuth's mind. Renee had, no doubt, told them a suave but completely untruthful story. Otherwise, why would he be afraid of the police?

Nancy was now confused as to whether or not Helene and Henri Fontaine were innocent. Instinct told her they were blameless, but the evidence seemed to be contradictory.

Nancy's thoughts returned to Ned. What was he doing? Had Renee returned to the house or made his getaway at once?

Ned, a quarter of a mile away, was worrying about Nancy. When he had reached the farmhouse, Renee had not been in sight. Ned had pounded on the door, but there had been no response. He had entered the building and searched it thoroughly, but had found no one.

As Ned went outdoors, he was amazed to see Renee hurrying up the lane.

"I'd hoped to find you here!" the man said excitedly. "Your wife's had an accident down the road. I'm going to phone the police!"

As Ned stood stunned, realizing Renee meant Nancy, the man dashed into the house. Ned was torn between a desire to get more details about the accident and a wish to help Nancy immediately. Deciding on the second move, he ran down the lane and turned to the highway.

After sprinting nearly half a mile, Ned stopped. He suddenly realized that Renee could not possibly have come this far and then return to the farmhouse in the length of time that had elapsed.

"Maybe someone came along and took Nancy to town," he concluded.

Or perhaps Renee's story had been a hoax! The only way to find out was to question him.

Turning, Ned ran back down the highway. While he was still some distance from the lane, he saw a black sedan pull out of it and speed off.

Ned was not close enough to read the license number, but he could see that there were four people in the vehicle. In the rear seat sat a blond young man and a girl with dark hair.

"The Fontaines!" Ned cried out involuntarily. "They *had been* prisoners in that farmhouse after all! But where had they been hidden?"

Ned wondered whether Renee had been in the sedan. He ran to the house and knocked loudly. No one answered, so he went inside. Renee was not anywhere on the first floor. The bedrooms also were empty.

"I'll phone the police," Ned decided. "Maybe Nancy did reach headquarters after all."

Finding a phone in one of the bedrooms, he called quickly. "Has Nancy Drew come in to see you?" he asked Captain Crane.

The officer said he had not seen the girl but would ask the other men on duty at headquarters. In a few moments he returned to the phone.

"Miss Drew is not here."

Ned quickly told his story, saying finally, "I'm afraid Nancy may have been kidnapped."

"Do you want me to send out an alarm for the black sedan?" the captain asked.

"Yes," Ned replied, "and I would like some police out here to help me hunt for Nancy."

By this time dusk had fallen. The frantic youth began to visualize Nancy in the hands of the ruthless smugglers. As he tried to put the horrifying thought out of his mind, a car turned into the lane. With a sense of relief, Ned saw a red blinking light on its roof. The police!

Two men had been sent. One of them was Officer Donovan. Ned told them of his and Nancy's second meeting with Renee.

"He tricked me into leaving the house with his story of an accident. Then he escaped by car with three other people," Ned finished.

"Looks bad!" said Donovan. "Suppose we start our search where Miss Drew began her walk through the woods to your car."

Ned led the way. It had grown almost dark and the men had to use their flashlights to pick up the trail. They stopped and searched carefully at the scuffle-marked spot where Nancy had encountered Renee.

"From here, only a man's footprints go in this direction," Donovan pointed out. "Looks as if he was pulling something. I'd say your friend was dragged from here."

"Then she can't be far away!" Ned cried. "Renee isn't a husky man and couldn't have dragged Nancy far. Maybe he was heading for my car. I left it not far from here."

About a hundred yards farther on they came to the place where Ned had left his car, but it was not there. Tire marks indicated that it had been driven down the road. Quickly Ned and the two policemen followed the tread marks.

Presently they came to a place where a car had been driven off the dusty thoroughfare and into the woods. Ned's heart sank. What was he going to find when they reached his car?

They had not gone far when the tracks of the automobile stopped. This could mean only that the car had been backed out again.

"Nancy's kidnappers drove in here temporarily, probably to avoid some passing car," Ned said.

Donovan laid a hand on the young man's shoulder. "Don't be so sure of that," he said. "A car might have pulled in here for a number of reasons."

They pushed farther along the road. After a few hundred yards they came to a second trail that led into the woods. Hopefully, the searchers turned in and followed it.

Suddenly the flashlight beam picked up the outline of an automobile. But upon closer inspection they found it to be just a rusted car that apparently had been junked some time ago.

Ned and the officers retraced their steps and continued the search. The road turned almost back on itself. It occurred to Ned that if Renee had kidnapped Nancy, he could have hidden her and the car temporarily. A shortcut back through the woods could explain the speed with which he had reached the lane to his farmhouse.

At this moment the flashlight's beam showed a car a short distance ahead.

"That's mine!" Ned shouted, pointing toward the cream-colored convertible. "Nancy! Nancy!"

The youth ran to the car and yanked open the

door. On the floor behind the front seat lay Nancy. Ned untied her and removed the gag.

"Oh, Nancy, are you all right?" he asked fearfully.

"Y-yes, Ned," she said in a daze. After several deep breaths she was able to tell her story. She hobbled around to restore circulation to her arms and legs.

"This is a fine end to my plan for a nice ride and dinner this evening," Ned said.

"I'm sorry, Ned."

Ned suggested that they start for home at once and stop in a restaurant on the way.

"But I'm a sight," Nancy protested. "I couldn't go anywhere to dinner. I'll tell you what. There must be some food at the farmhouse. Let's go up there and help ourselves. Then we can do a little investigating in the house."

Ned shook his head in amazement. Turning to the policemen, he said, "Nancy Drew never gives up until she has solved a case!"

They all climbed into the car and Ned drove back to the farmhouse. Donovan contacted Captain Crane and made a report. The captain ordered him to guard the farmhouse overnight. The other officer was to return to headquarters as soon as the house had been investigated.

Ned had hoped Nancy would take it easy, but she insisted that what she needed was exercise.

Together they opened several cans of food they found on a shelf, and warmed the contents. The police officers, who had eaten earlier, inspected the grounds.

When the improvised meal was finished, Nancy accompanied the officers on their investigation of the house. Upstairs, they checked the bedrooms one by one. Finally Nancy asked to borrow Officer Donovan's flashlight.

"All right," Donovan said, handing it to her. "I'd like to watch a girl detective work. But would you mind telling me why you need it?"

Nancy said that if the missing Fontaines had been at the house, Helene probably would have practiced her dancing. She was searching for signs of this.

"Ballet dancers," Nancy explained, "never let a day go by without working. They have to keep their muscles in perfect condition."

Nancy got down on her hands and knees and began examining the floor. Suddenly she stopped.

"Look here!" she cried excitedly. "This floor has been waxed recently. And see these long slide marks and rounded dents in the waxed surface? These were made by toe shoes."

"Hmmm," said Donovan. "Guess you're right. But say, can these folks dance without music?"

"Why certainly," Nancy said.

Just then Ned walked into the room. "I have a clue for you, Nancy!" he said.

The young man had called the telephone company and obtained the name of the party under which the farmhouse phone was listed.

"Does the name Raymond Bull mean anything to you?" he asked.

"Indeed it does!" Nancy replied. "He's the Frenchman who was on the plane from New York to River Heights with Mr. Koff and me."

"Could it be an alias of Renee's?" Ned asked.

"That's possible."

Further search of the house disclosed no clues that would indicate the destination of the fugitives or give any inkling of their plans. The young people said good night to Donovan and drove the other officer back to headquarters.

At the police station, Nancy stopped to find out whether Mrs. Judson had confessed or whether she had had any suspicious callers.

Captain Crane shook his head. "We've tried to get Mrs. Judson to talk, but she refuses."

"Did you search her handbag and other personal belongings?" Nancy asked.

"Oh, yes," Captain Crane replied. "One of our matrons handled that, but she found nothing of any use in the case." The captain went on to say that there had been no report on the black sedan and its occupants.

It was nearly midnight when Nancy and Ned reached River Heights. Nancy was weary and slept late the following morning. As she awakened, the young sleuth found herself looking up into the faces of Hannah Gruen, Bess, and George.

"Well, sleepyhead," George said, seating herself on the edge of Nancy's four-poster. "Tell us everything!"

The girls listened attentively. After Nancy had eaten her breakfast, she told her friends she was heading back to the farmhouse in Brandon. "This time I'm going to search the barn from top to bottom," she declared. "Want to join me?"

"Wouldn't miss it," George declared.

Bess was hesitant until Nancy assured her that the place was being guarded by the police.

When the girls reached Renee's hideout, Officer Donovan welcomed Nancy with a wide smile.

Nancy introduced her friends and explained that they were going to search the barn for clues. The three entered the rickety building and found that the main floor contained nothing but a few pieces of obsolete machinery.

"Hayloft next," said George.

Working in various locations of the loft, they began pulling the loose hay apart. Suddenly Nancy exclaimed, "Girls, here's a briefcase hidden in the hay."

The cousins rushed over. "Is it Mr. Koff's?" Bess asked excitedly.

CHAPTER XIX

Desperate Measures

WITH Bess and George waiting eagerly, Nancy looked inside the briefcase and exclaimed, "This is Mr. Koff's, all right! Here's his full name and address pasted on the inside."

Bess, peering over Nancy's shoulder, suddenly cried out, "Oh, Nancy, put it down!"

"Why?" George demanded.

"Because," Bess told her fearfully, "there's a note that says, " 'Do not read the contents or you will die!' ''

"That's ridiculous," George said in disgust. "Nancy, you aren't going to let that stop you, are you?"

"Not that threat," Nancy replied, "because I doubt that Mr. Koff wrote it. I would return the briefcase to him without looking at the letters except for one thing."

"What's that?"

Nancy picked up an envelope on which had been scrawled *from Red Buzby*.

"Remember the red-haired man?" she asked. "I think this is a real clue. I vote we take the briefcase into the house and read every single letter—if we can. They may be in Centrovian."

The girls climbed down the hayloft ladder and went to the house. Nancy looked around for Officer Donovan to tell him what she was going to do, but the guard was not in sight.

"Phew! What a strong odor of kerosene!" Bess said. "What would that policeman be doing with kerosene?"

Nancy shrugged. She was too interested in getting at the letters to care.

The first floor of the house had only one small table in the kitchen, so the three girls went upstairs to the front room and spread out the contents of the briefcase on the bed. They had been written in French and Nancy translated one after another. She could readily see why Mr. Koff had not wanted them to fall into enemy hands. The letters hinted at drastic movements of the underground against the Centrovian occupation.

Suddenly George interrupted Nancy. "Here's a typed carbon of one in English signed *Buzby*." She read it aloud:

Dear Pal, I have a plan worked out for selling these letters to those guys in Europe. It should bring us plenty in good American dollars.

"How wicked!" Bess exclaimed.

Nancy nodded. "I'm glad we located these letters before they were sold."

She and her friends found several other notations signed by Buzby. One of these, apparently an answer to some inquiry that had been made, read:

Don't worry. Nobody will ever find out who Judson is. 10561-B-24.

"The mysterious number again!" Bess exclaimed. "Whatever does it mean?"

"I have an idea," said Nancy, "and if I'm right the number will go a long way toward tying this mystery together."

She picked up the telephone and called her father, who was working in his study at home. After reporting her discovery to him, she said, "Will you please call the French embassy and ask whether 10561-B-24 could have been a passport number, and if so, to whom it was issued?"

"I'll do it right away," the lawyer assured her.

As Nancy hung up and turned around, the girls heard a loud clattering in the hall below and went to the stairway to investigate.

Henri and Helene Fontaine were rushing up the steps!

"Nancy!" the dancers cried and Helene hugged her friend fervently. "Bess! George! We're so glad to see you!"

The girls were speechless, but finally Bess blurted out, "You—you're not smugglers? You didn't run away?"

"We were spirited away," Helene replied. "We were told how that dreadful man Renee had accused us of stealing the painting with the scarlet slippers."

"And also of stealing a fortune in jewels," Henri added.

"Tell us everything," Nancy begged, leading the way into the room. "It's so good to see you."

As Henri began to talk, Bess went to close the door. The odor of kerosene was very strong now. Again she wondered what Officer Donovan was doing with it.

"Helene and I," said Henri, "have been held prisoners ever since leaving Ned's cabin. We were brought here first by two men named Red Buzby and Duparc."

"Buzby!" Nancy exclaimed. "He's the one who probably stole the briefcase and planned to sell the letters! But go on."

Henri continued, "It seems Renee had rented this place, but Buzby was using it while Renee was off on a false lead Red had given him. The day after we arrived here, Buzby got word that Renee was returning in a rage, so we were taken to another deserted farmhouse located not far from here."

"Then it wasn't you two who were in the car that Ned saw leaving here yesterday," Nancy said.

"No. We were already at the other farmhouse. We managed to escape a little while ago, when we found our guard had gone off duty."

Helene took up the story. "We phoned your house at once. When Hannah Gruen told us that you were here, we were fearful for your safety and came right over."

Nancy was touched deeply by their loyalty. "If your kidnappers come here, they'll be met by a policeman," she said. "Now please go on with the story. But first, I want to tell you that these papers are Mr. Koff's. I found this briefcase."

"How wonderful!" Helene exclaimed. Then she said, "Henri and I were so happy at the Nickerson lodge. Then late one afternoon two strange men came to the door—Buzby and Duparc. They threatened us with guns and there was nothing we could do but follow them to a car. There was no time to leave a note."

Helene said that she had phoned Nancy from the farmhouse, but Buzby had caught her. He had already sent a woman friend to the telegraph office with a fake message for Nancy.

Henri smiled slightly. "But we told Buzby that Nancy knew about the smuggling racket and was closing in on the gang."

"Then what happened?" George prompted.

"They sneered and said nobody could prove them guilty. But since we were never going to be free, they would tell us the whole story."

The Fontaines said that Renee and Amien were partners in the theft of the Centrovian jewels from the underground and in the smuggling racket. They had worked on it for months and everything had gone smoothly. First the bisque figurines were sent to the United States, then eleven of the paintings.

"But before the last picture was ready to be shipped," said Henri, "Amien double-crossed Renee. He secretly sent the portrait with the scarlet slippers. Under the paint was a good part of the loot. He was in league with a New York art dealer named Duparc. Amien came to this country to share the money from the sale of the jewels with Duparc."

"And left Renee out?" Bess asked.

"Yes. Duparc is Amien's brother-in-law. He also uses the name Warte."

Nancy said excitedly, "I see how you Fontaines figured in it. Amien sent you the warning note in France to make you flee and thus look guilty, so Renee wouldn't suspect his partner of double-crossing him."

"Exactly." Henri nodded. "But after a while, when no money came to Renee from the sale of jewels, he became suspicious and sailed for the United States. When he learned Duparc had disappeared, he was convinced he had been cheated and set out to find Amien and Duparc and us."

George said, "I don't see where Buzby figures in the deal."

Henri explained that Buzby was serving both sides and getting money from everyone. Actually, he was a small-time racketeer who was related to Mrs. Amien, alias Mrs. Judson.

"Buzby," said Henri, "acted as a spy for Amien. When Amien learned that Renee was in the United States, he sent Red Buzby to meet him. He found Renee eager to catch up with his crooked partner and Buzby assured him he knew just where to find Raoul Amien. But he led Renee on a merry chase to keep him from finding Amien."

"But I suppose," said Nancy, "that Renee caught on."

"Yes. He accused Buzby of tricking him."

"What did Buzby do then?" Bess asked.

Henri said that Buzby's glib tongue and quick brain had saved him. He told Renee he knew all about the man's crooked operations in France, that the authorities there were looking for him, and that he could make plenty of trouble for Renee.

"Buzby is a bad one," Helene said. "Renee tried to get away from him. He began to look for Amien himself and trailed him to River Heights. At this point Amien became desperate and sent a second note to Henri and me to flee."

"But that was where his plan went wrong," George remarked. "Nancy stepped into the picture and really whisked you folks out of sight, which frightened Amien."

As George finished speaking and Henri said, "That is true," Nancy suddenly sniffed. Then she glanced toward the sill of the closed door. *Smoke was seeping into the room!*

Nancy jumped to the door. Flinging it open, she found the hall filled with smoke.

"The house is on fire!" she cried in dismay.

Nancy could now hear flames crackling below. She slammed the door shut and rushed to the window, looking for a means of escape. To her horror, she discovered that the grass, bushes, and side of the house were ablaze.

"Oh, what will we do?" Bess wailed.

The others ran from room to room and glanced outside. A wide band of fire completely encircled the house!

"We must try the stairs," Henri ordered.

Covering their faces with handkerchiefs, the group tried to descend the steps, but flames and smoke drove them back. The first floor of the old wooden structure was completely ablaze. Escape down the stairs was impossible.

"The kerosene!" Nancy thought ruefully. "Someone soaked the premises inside and out and made an inferno of this place."

"The house is on fire!" Nancy cried.

As she dashed back into the bedroom, where the briefcase and letters lay, she wondered about Officer Donovan. He must have been knocked out! Her suspicions were confirmed a moment later when, through the haze outside, she saw him lying at the edge of the woods.

"Nancy, oh Nancy, we'll die!" Bess murmured, clinging to her friend.

With escape cut off, it seemed as if Bess might be right!

CHAPTER XX

Grand Finale

HENRI had dashed to the telephone to summon help, but the wires had been cut.

"There's only one chance for escape!" Nancy declared. "We'll have to make a rope out of sheets and blankets, and swing out the window beyond the flames!"

As she and George dashed to a bed, Helene, standing near a window, cried, "Renee is outside!"

Henri rushed to her side and peered below. "And that's Red Buzby with him!"

"Help! Help!" Bess screamed.

The men looked up and sneered. Turning on their heels, they went down the lane.

"They can't run off and leave us!" Bess wailed frantically.

There was no doubt now in Nancy's mind that

the men had purposely set the fire after knocking out Officer Donovan. But there was no time for reflection. Nancy and the others tore the bed sheets and knotted them together.

One end of the life line was tied securely to a leg of the bed, which was shoved close to the window. At this moment they heard a car pull away and concluded that Renee and Buzby had gone off.

"George," said Nancy, "suppose you climb out first."

The athletic girl gripped the rope, started down the side of the building, then kicked herself away from it. She half leaped, half fell, safely to the ground, just beyond the burning area of grass.

George held onto the end of the line to keep it from falling into the flames and swung it over a branch of a scorched maple nearby. She held it taut as Bess swung hand over hand to safety. Helene followed, then Nancy, the papers from Koff's briefcase stuffed in her pockets, and finally Henri.

No sooner had the young man jumped to the ground than the whole farmhouse seemed to collapse. The group was hardly conscious of the intense heat from the flames as, in relief, they hugged one another, alternately laughing and crying hysterically. Their faces were black with soot and the smoke made their eyes smart.

"Let's go!" Bess urged. "I can't get away from here fast enough."

Suddenly Nancy remembered Officer Donovan. They found him at the edge of the woods. The guard was just regaining consciousness.

A car turned into the lane at that moment. "Oh, it must be those dreadful men!" Bess cried. "We'd better hide, so they can't harm us!"

Nancy agreed but not for the reason Bess had given. She felt that it would be an excellent opportunity to capture Buzby and Renee.

To Bess's relief, the occupant of the car was Ned Nickerson. As he leaped to the ground, Nancy and the others stepped out from hiding. Ned looked at the Fontaines as if he were seeing two ghosts. Then he stared at the disheveled group and at the burning farmhouse.

"Whatever happened?" he asked.

Explanations were quickly given. Then Nancy asked how Ned knew where they were.

"I called your house, Nancy, to find out how you felt today," the young man replied. "Your father answered. He said you were here and that he had been trying to get you on the phone, but there was no answer. He seemed quite concerned, so I offered to come and find you."

"Did Dad say why he was trying to get me?" Nancy asked.

Ned smiled. "He has solved part of your mystery, Nancy. He found out from the French embassy that 10561-B-24 is the number of the passport issued to Raoul Amien."

"Oh, Nancy, you were right!" George declared. "Now Judson can't deny who he really is!"

Nancy felt that they should notify the fire department and the police at once.

"Maybe the barn can be saved," she said. "And furthermore, I have a hunch Renee and Buzby will come back here to see the result of their horrible deed."

Officer Donovan said he would radio headquarters and the fire department from the police car. He set off to the spot in the woods where the sedan had been secreted.

"The rest of us can hide until the police come," Nancy said. "If Renee and Buzby should show up, you boys can take care of them."

"Nothing would please me better," said Ned, and Henri added, "Just let me get my hands on either one of them!"

Shortly afterward, Officer Donovan joined the group. He said that the police and fire trucks would be there immediately. Then he told them about his being slugged.

"I kept smelling kerosene and was trying to investigate where it was coming from when someone came up from behind and hit me on the head."

Suddenly Ned grabbed Nancy's arm and pointed. "Sh!" he warned the group.

Coming from the woods at the back of the barn were Renee and Buzby!

Ned and Henri, crouching low, cautiously inched their way forward. When the men were almost opposite them, they leaped from their hiding place and hurled themselves at the two suspects. The ensuing fight was of short duration. While Ned and Henri held Renee and Buzby in viselike grips, Officer Donovan handcuffed the prisoners.

Renee began to whine. "You have no right to hold me. I haven't done anything. This is my home that burned down. You ought to have a little sympathy instead of putting handcuffs on me."

"One or both of you men set fire to the house and tried to burn it down with us in it," Nancy challenged.

Both prisoners vehemently denied the charge.

"Anyway, there is another serious charge against you, Buzby, which you can't deny," declared Henri. "Kidnapping!"

"And now, Buzby," said Nancy, "suppose you tell us where Raoul Amien is."

Buzby smirked. "What would it be worth to you to know? My price is high."

Nancy looked at the man in disgust. "Right

now, you're not in a very good bargaining position," she said. "We'll find out soon enough. Mrs. Amien is in jail, and when she finds out you people are prisoners, she'll tell us where her husband is."

At that moment they heard the sound of fire sirens and presently several pieces of apparatus pulled into the lane. Within fifteen minutes the fire was under control.

Captain Crane arrived in a police car with several officers. The men praised Nancy and all her friends for their part in the capture of Renee and Buzby. Captain Crane said that Mrs. Amien had broken down and given her husband's address. Officers had been sent to get him.

"Suppose we go back to headquarters and try to get statements from the whole gang," the captain suggested. Then he read the captives their rights.

He invited Nancy to ride with him and the two prisoners, who would be handcuffed to another officer in the rear seat of his car.

"You probably have a few questions to ask them," he said, a twinkle in his eye.

Nancy was glad for this opportunity. When she brought up the subject of Mr. Koff's briefcase, Buzby admitted having been on the plane and switching cases while pretending to comfort the distraught man.

"I had heard that Koff was working for the Centrovian underground," said Buzby, "and when he started making a fuss on the plane, I was sure he had some valuable information in his briefcase. So I decided to get it. My own brief-case was almost a duplicate of his, so it was easy to make the switch."

Nancy then asked if he and Amien, alias Judson, had worked the scheme of trying to get money from Mr. Koff. Buzby confessed that the two had worked it out together, but the plan had failed when Koff had turned the matter over to Mr. Drew.

Nancy learned also that it was Amien who had trailed Koff and his daughter Millie to Cliffwood. Also, it was Amien's idea to use his passport number under stamps as an identification mark on all correspondence between members of the conspiracy. Anyone sending phony orders could be detected.

The suspect was amazed to learn that one of the slips containing the number had been found in the figurine. He surmised that it had been slipped in accidentally when the jewels were being secreted.

"You're too smart, Miss Drew," he said. "But one of these days you'll come across somebody you won't be able to outsmart!"

Nancy ignored the remark and asked if it were

Buzby and Duparc who had sold the figurines and paintings in which the jewels had been smuggled to the United States.

"Yeah," said Buzby. "We saw a way to make a few extra bucks and get rid of the hot paintings, too."

He glared in hatred at Nancy when she told him that the smugglers had failed to remove a few of the jewels.

"Who called my father that night, pretending to be Koff, and asked him to go to New York?" Nancy asked.

"Duparc," Buzby answered. "He's good at imitating voices and was able to convince your father he was Koff."

Captain Crane parked the police car in front of headquarters and they all went inside. Mr. and Mrs. Amien, alias Judson, were waiting. Renee sprang at the husband like a cat but was quickly dragged away.

Amien and his wife looked balefully at Nancy, but remained quiet and finally answered the questions put to them. Nancy learned that it was Amien who had written all the threatening notes, both to the Fontaines and to her.

Finally, Nancy turned to Mrs. Judson and asked, "What was your part in this business?"

"My husband forced me to do all sorts of things," she replied. "He made me write the anonymous notes to the parents of the dancing school kids. One day when I went over to River Heights to check with Red Buzby, I decided to steal the scarlet slippers."

"That was your husband's idea, too?" Nancy asked.

"No," Mrs. Amien admitted. "That was my own idea. I heard my husband say to Duparc that the jewels had been hidden in the scarlet slippers. I didn't know he meant the ones in the portrait, so when I saw the pair on the wall of the dancing school, I decided to take them. Of course there wasn't anything in the slippers."

Before Nancy and her friends left headquarters, Renee and Buzby admitted setting fire to the farmhouse. The police had taken Duparc into custody. He had been trying to make a getaway with the man and woman Ned had thought were the Fontaines. They were part of the smuggling ring. The foreign authorities had already been notified to investigate Amien's Parisian friend who had sent the letter Mrs. Amien had picked up at the River Heights post office.

The next day, the River Heights *Gazette* and newspapers all over the country featured the story of Nancy Drew and the mystery of the scarlet slippers. The young detective was deluged with telephone calls and wires.

One call made her smile broadly. It came from

Mrs. Parsons who said, "Nancy, even if you couldn't dance a step, I would have had you in our charity show. Why, my dear, you're the talk of the town!"

Nancy was glad to escape for a short time to the Nickerson cabin on Cedar Lake. Here the Fontaines, Mr. Koff and Millie, Bess, George, and Ned held a private celebration of their own. At the party Nancy found herself wondering when another mystery would come along. She had no way of knowing that within a very short time she would be involved in *The Witch Tree Symbol*.

Nancy's thoughts were interrupted when she realized that Henri and Helene were thanking her and her friends over and over again for what they had done.

"You'll never know how grateful we are," Helene declared. "You saved our lives, our reputation, and our school. And you've done a great service for the struggling, freedom-loving people of Centrovia."

"Do you think you'll ever go back to Centrovia?" Bess asked them.

The Fontaines smiled and Henri said, "Maybe someday to visit, after peace is restored. But now we would like to become citizens of your grand country."

"How wonderful!" Bess exclaimed.

"And," Helene added, tears in her eyes, "we

could never think of leaving such a fine friend as you, Nancy Drew. And you, Bess and George, you're just marvelous, too."

Henri nodded and said, "Nancy, I haven't forgotten my promise of a gift to you to show my appreciation. I shall finish your portrait and it will be my finest work."

"And it should be titled," Ned said, smiling at Nancy, "America's Loveliest Sleuth."

ORDER FORM

NANCY DREW
MYSTERY SERIES

by Carolyn Keene

55 TITLES AT YOUR BOOKSELLER OR
COMPLETE THIS HANDY COUPON AND MAIL TO:

GROSSET & DUNLAP, INC.
P.O. Box 941, Madison Square Post Office, New York, N.Y. 10010

Please send me the Nancy Drew Mystery Book(s) checked below @ $2.95 each, plus 25¢ per book postage and handling. My check or money order for $_____ is enclosed. (Please do not send cash.)

☐ 1.	Secret of the Old Clock	9501-7	
☐ 2.	Hidden Staircase	9502-5	
☐ 3.	Bungalow Mystery	9503-3	
☐ 4.	Mystery at Lilac Inn	9504-1	
☐ 5.	Secret of Shadow Ranch	9505-X	
☐ 6.	Secret of Red Gate Farm	9506-8	
☐ 7.	Clue in the Diary	9507-6	
☐ 8.	Nancy's Mysterious Letter	9508-4	
☐ 9.	The Sign of the Twisted Candles	9509-2	
☐ 10.	Password to Larkspur Lane	9510-6	
☐ 11.	Clue of the Broken Locket	9511-4	
☐ 12.	The Message in the Hollow Oak	9512-2	
☐ 13.	Mystery of the Ivory Charm	9513-0	
☐ 14.	The Whispering Statue	9514-9	
☐ 15.	Haunted Bridge	9515-7	
☐ 16.	Clue of the Tapping Heels	9516-5	
☐ 17.	Mystery of the Brass Bound Trunk	9517-3	
☐ 18.	Mystery at Moss-Covered Mansion	9518-1	
☐ 19.	Quest of the Missing Map	9519-X	
☐ 20.	Clue in the Jewel Box	9520-3	
☐ 21.	The Secret in the Old Attic	9521-1	
☐ 22.	Clue in the Crumbling Wall	9522-X	
☐ 23.	Mystery of the Tolling Bell	9523-8	
☐ 24.	Clue in the Old Album	9524-6	
☐ 25.	Ghost of Blackwood Hall	9525-4	
☐ 26.	Clue of the Leaning Chimney	9526-2	
☐ 27.	Secret of the Wooden Lady	9527-0	

☐ 28.	The Clue of the Black Keys	9528-9	
☐ 29.	Mystery at the Ski Jump	9529-7	
☐ 30.	Clue of the Velvet Mask	9530-0	
☐ 31.	Ringmaster's Secret	9531-9	
☐ 32.	Scarlet Slipper Mystery	9532-7	
☐ 33.	Witch Tree Symbol	9533-5	
☐ 34.	Hidden Window Mystery	9534-3	
☐ 35.	Haunted Showboat	9535-1	
☐ 36.	Secret of the Golden Pavilion	9536-X	
☐ 37.	Clue in the Old Stagecoach	9537-8	
☐ 38.	Mystery of the Fire Dragon	9538-6	
☐ 39.	Clue of the Dancing Puppet	9539-4	
☐ 40.	Moonstone Castle Mystery	9540-8	
☐ 41.	Clue of the Whistling Bagpipes	9541-6	
☐ 42.	Phantom of Pine Hill	9542-4	
☐ 43.	Mystery of the 99 Steps	9543-2	
☐ 44.	Clue in the Crossword Cipher	9544-0	
☐ 45.	Spider Sapphire Mystery	9545-9	
☐ 46.	The Invisible Intruder	9546-7	
☐ 47.	The Mysterious Mannequin	9547-5	
☐ 48.	The Crooked Banister	9548-3	
☐ 49.	The Secret of Mirror Bay	9549-1	
☐ 50.	The Double Jinx Mystery	9550-5	
☐ 51.	Mystery of the Glowing Eye	9551-3	
☐ 52.	The Secret of the Forgotten City	9552-1	
☐ 53.	The Sky Phantom	9553-X	
☐ 54.	The Strange Message in the Parchment	9554-8	
☐ 55	Mystery of Crocodile Island	9555-6	

SHIP TO:

NAME _____
(please print)

ADDRESS _____

CITY _____ STATE _____ ZIP _____

Printed in U.S.A.   **Please do not send cash.**